Vanquished

Enslaved, Book 1

Katie Clark

I0673984

Vanquished

Contact Information: titleadmin@pelicanbookgroup.com

Scripture quotations, unless otherwise indicated are taken from the King James translation, public domain.

Cover Art by Nicola Martinez

Watershed Books, a division of Pelican Ventures, LLC
www.pelicanbookgroup.com PO Box 1738 *Aztec, NM * 87410

Watershed Books praise and splash logo is a trademark of Pelican Ventures, LLC

Publishing History
First Watershed Edition, 2014
Paperback Edition ISBN 978-1-61116-401-5
Electronic Edition ISBN 978-1-61116-400-8
Published in the United States of America

Dedication

Lovingly dedicated to all those people who made me
believe that I could.

Praise

[Vanquished is] an emotional and unique take on a world of haves vs. have-nots that will pull you in from the very first page. ~ Kelly Hashway, author of *Touch of Death*

1

The old hospital looms in front of me like some ancient castle from the Early Days. This is where they keep people with the mutation. My heart races at the thought of going inside.

I've never been in a hospital before. In fact, I've never been in a building that big at all. I wish I'd taken Jamie's offer to come with me or had come with Dad last night. I wish that Mom hadn't gotten the mutation at all.

I take a deep breath and push through the double doors.

The quiet lobby area is dim, lit by a few small windows and a couple of glowing lamps. I knew the hospital gets extra electricity allowance, but I've almost never seen anyone use manufactured lighting during the day. I'm awed by the sight. In front of me is an abandoned office area, and to my right is an old cafeteria. A sign dangles over the counter by one chain. It seems like someone would have taken it down by now.

I make a split decision and yank it down. Chains clatter as they plunge to the floor. It stays on the ground, and I turn back to the main lobby. My heartbeat calms at regaining this tiny bit of control.

Beyond the cafeteria, several signs hang on the wall. One points me to the stairs.

My dad said Mom was on the third floor. Back in

the Early Days, they fought the mutation with chemotherapy drugs and something called radiation. We don't have those things anymore, so we fight it with fruits, vegetables, and herbs. Sometimes it works, but most of the time it doesn't. I don't want to think about what this means for Mom.

The door to the stairs is beside the old elevator shafts. I reach out and feel the cool metal doors. They reflect my image back to me, but I don't pay attention to that. I've seen enough of my short blond hair and not-so-tall stature, but I've never actually seen elevators before. I wish the doors would open, and I could peek inside. Riding up to the third floor would be even better, but no one has enough electricity allowance to run elevators, not even the hospital I guess.

I make the climb to the third floor without even getting winded, and more manufactured lighting greets me. Long bulbs line the ceiling. These lights are brighter than the lamps downstairs, and they make an odd buzzing noise. I stumbled into a beehive once, and the angry bees buzzed a lot like the lights.

There are so many rooms down the long hallway, I can't imagine there would ever be enough sick people to fill them all, but then I remember what they tell us about the Early Days. There were a lot more people back then. Now there are so few people I think we could all fit in this hospital together. How would it feel to be around so many people, all the time? Would it feel crowded? I don't think so. I think it would feel safe.

The hallway is empty, but a faint beeping comes from down the hall. I pass an old desk on my way toward the beeping. A dumpy computer sits on the desk. People still have those?

I pass one door, two doors, and then an irritated voice stops me in my tracks.

"We could give her chemo at the onset to slow things down a bit, and then start the natural healing. The least we can do is to give her a fighting chance. She's a Middle, after all." It's a woman's voice, coming from the room with the faint beeping. Her tone is hushed and angry.

I look at the piece of paper that's been tacked to the wall outside the room.

Maya Norfolk.

I suck in a tight breath. They're talking about Mom? What do they mean by 'a fighting chance'? My heart picks up speed, and I step closer to the room, careful to stay out of view.

"It takes time to get approval for chemo drugs, and what if she talks? Everyone who gets the mutation will start demanding them. What's her occupation?" It's a man's voice, and he sounds just as angry.

Papers shuffle and the woman says, "Professor at the military academy. I say we do it. She knows how to keep secrets if she's worked in the military. What chance does she have otherwise?"

The pause in conversation is excruciating as Mom's life hangs in the balance. Meanwhile my mind spins. Chemo drugs? They're not even supposed to exist. How can they be talking about this so casually? Have the rest of us been lied to all this time?

"Do you need some help?"

I jerk around, my heart thumping like the rain during a torrential downpour. A boy stands in front of me. He doesn't look much older than my seventeen years, but definitely old enough to have taken the Test.

"I was looking for my mom's room," I say quickly. "I've never been here before." I hope that sounded innocent and confused, and not like I'm scared to be caught eavesdropping.

"What's her name?" His dark hair is short, but it has a little curl to it. His chocolaty brown eyes aren't suspicious, not like they'd be if he suspected me of listening to the doctors.

"It's Maya Norfolk. I think this is her room, but I wasn't sure if I was allowed to just walk in."

He smiles kindly. "People are usually nervous, but you don't have to be. You can go on in." His smile makes his cheeks puff out like he's carrying an apple in each one. I could watch him smile all day.

"Thanks," I force myself to look down.

When I turn around, two people are coming out. The doctors, obviously.

"This is Maya Norfolk's daughter," the boy says. "What's your name, miss?"

I lick my lips. Do the doctors suspect I heard any part of their conversation? "Hana. I'm Hana Norfolk."

The woman smiles. "It's nice to meet you, Hana. I'm Dr. Lane, and this is Dr. Bentford. We'll be taking care of your mom." She sticks her hand out.

I've never shaken someone's hand before—I thought it was a tradition that went out with the Early Days. Her hand is warm and rough, and she pumps my hand up and down once. Dr. Bentford reaches forward for his turn and gives my hand a half dozen fast shakes.

People who don't know each other don't typically touch. It feels very strange.

"Nice to meet you," I mumble. "I guess I'll go in now." No one stops me or questions me, and I slip into

Mom's room. It's darker in here, but then I see the curtains. They're drawn, and the light is switched off. My mom is sleeping.

A bed sits in the middle of the room, and there are two chairs on either side of it. A pole stands beside the bed with a bag of fluid. It drips into a long tube that goes into Mom's hand. The bag hangs freely, not plugged up to electricity. I wonder what makes the water run.

She still looks like Mom. The mutation hasn't eaten away her body yet. She hasn't lost weight or her coloring. Back in the Early Days people even lost their hair, but that was from the chemo drugs, not the mutation. I touch her hair softly, remembering all the times she held my hair for me when I was little and got sick. She would give me a cup of water afterward, and then brush my hair. That's always been my favorite— getting my hair brushed.

I look at her hair again, coming out of my fog. Would Mom care if she lost her hair? No, I don't think so. I got that from her, not caring about my looks all that much. Besides, she most likely won't lose her hair anyway. Only if they decide to go ahead with chemotherapy.

Chemo drugs. I take a shaky breath and sit in one of the rickety chairs. Do chemotherapy drugs really still exist? If so, why don't they give them to everyone? The man had said they needed approval for them, and Mom would have to keep it a secret. None of that makes sense to me.

A soft rap comes from behind the door, and the boy from the hallway comes in with a glass of water. "I wasn't sure how long you'd be here," he says. "You might get thirsty."

I take the glass and smile. "Thanks."

He pauses like he wants to say more. "I'm sorry about the diagnosis. The mutation is always hard to hear."

I nod and look down. It *is* hard to hear. Everyone knows it's almost a death sentence. Tears burn my eyes and I blink them away. My mom can't die.

"If you need something just let me know," he says. "I'll do anything I can to help. And if you have any questions, I'm happy to get the doctors for you."

My head bobs up and down like a puppet's. "Sure. Thanks again." Talking is hard because I suddenly have a ball in my throat. I try to swallow it down, but it doesn't help.

"No problem. It was nice to meet you, Hana. I'll see you around." He retreats soundlessly, and I realize I didn't learn his name. He was very kind. I've never seen kindness like that in someone else's eyes. It was almost like he really cared. A thought sprints through my mind, almost gone before I recognize it. What would it be like to be around him all the time?

Why should he care about what happens to me or Mom? Maybe it's his job — part of his training. Maybe medics are supposed to help comfort those who are sick or injured.

I glance at the bag of fluids hanging on the pole. It looks like water, but of course, I wouldn't know. The fluids, along with the glass of water in my hands, make me realize the hospital must get extra water allowance too. That's good. Whoever made up the rules in the government must have known how it felt to have someone they loved in the hospital. They know how to take care of people who are hurting. Our small society may not have many resources, but we pool them and survive. The more you help the society, the more you are helped, in spite of the million rules we have to follow.

I narrow my eyes and bite my lip. If the Greaters do whatever's best for their citizens, could the chemo drugs help her? I watch Mom's chest move up and down, and a dull ache grows behind my eyes. What will I do if she dies? What will Dad do? What will happen to her?

My mind flashes back to their whispered conversation and an argument about life after death. That was when I was little, but I've never forgotten. I wipe my tears before they run down my face. My mom can't die. A brick wall goes up in my heart. If there are chemotherapy drugs somewhere, I'm going to find out. If there's help for Mom to be found, I'm going to find it.

2

"All of you in this class will be taking your Test in three weeks' time," Mrs. Sewell says. She stands in front of our small class and points to the chalkboard. "This is the list of occupations you will be vying for."

I don't even glance at the board, since I already know which occupation I hope to get. Really I'm just eager for Mrs. Sewell to finish up. This is the last class of the day, and I want to see Mom. I need to know she's OK, that she's hanging in there.

"I want you to take a good look, because we're going to be discussing each of these occupations today, and you're going to tell me why you want the job you choose. Later this week is the career fair, and I want you to be prepared."

A collective groan moves through the room.

Mrs. Sewell smiles and rolls her eyes. "Trust me. It's better to choose what you want to do with your life and to work toward it, than to let it be chosen for you. Or worse, not to Test at all."

That statement gets everyone quiet pretty fast. If a citizen chooses not to test, he is automatically demoted to Lesser for the rest of his life. The Lessers get less food and electricity than everyone else. We can barely survive as Middles—we don't want to try and make it as Lessers.

"Is that how you ended up teaching?" one of the students calls out playfully. It breaks the tension and everyone laughs.

Mrs. Sewell laughs, too, but shakes her head. "No, I always knew I wanted to teach. Is there anyone here who hopes to be a teacher?"

At first no one says anything. I glance around to see if anyone is brave enough to raise their hand. Finally, Bernadette Dobbs slips up a hand. "I'd like to teach, but I'd rather teach small kids, like the five and six year olds."

Mrs. Sewell nods. "Excellent! Who else knows what they want to do?"

I duck my head. I've never liked speaking in front of a group, but when Mrs. Sewell's eyes hone in on me I know she's going to call on me.

"Hana, what about you?"

Which is ridiculous, since she already knows what I want to do. I've talked with her about it more than once. I clear my throat. "I want to work in the government."

Immediately I hear chuckles from the others. My cheeks tingle, and I look at my notebook. I've doodled cats and birds all over the cover.

Mrs. Sewell puts up her hand to stop the murmurs. "Hana has a great plan. Tell us why you want to do this."

My mouth is suddenly as dry as the sidewalk when it hasn't rained in three weeks. "I want to help the Lessers."

There aren't any chuckles this time. In fact, there's no noise at all. You could hear a pin drop, as they used to say in the Early Days.

"Why would you want to help them?" someone asks.

I turn to Lilith Winters. "Why would you *not*? If

we had more Greaters and Middles, wouldn't the country be better as a whole? Why keep feeding the Lessers' bad habits? We can train them to do better—to be better. They're people too, you know."

Lilith opens her mouth—to argue, I'm sure—but Mrs. Sewell cuts her off. "Do you see how passionate Hana is about her future? It's best to choose something you can be equally as passionate about. Who else can tell me what they hope to do?"

Passionate? I've never thought of myself as passionate. I only want to help them. My mom told me that she gave a Lesser boy her lunch once. She said she was on a walk with her father when she was young, and they came to the fence around a Lesser city. She said the boy was so skinny she could see his bones, so she slipped him the cheese sandwich when her dad wasn't looking.

I've wanted to be like her ever since.

I turn back to the front of the class, but I can feel Lilith behind me, frowning. She's disliked me since we were fifteen. She told everyone in school that year that she hoped to marry my good friend, Keegan. She said she would sing, and Keegan would play his guitar. They would be stars. Keegan had ignored her completely that year, while he continued to hang out with me and Jamie.

Really, I don't know what she expected. The three of us were best friends. I don't understand why she thought she could change that.

After class she meets me in the hallway. Her hair is black and naturally curly. She wears it cut short, so her curls fly around her head wildly. Most of the boys say she's pretty. I guess I can see why, but she's meaner than anyone I've ever met.

"Why do you think you could ever even get a job in the government? You have to have special connections for jobs like that. You don't have those connections, especially since your dad is only the dean of the agricultural college." She pronounces each syllable of 'agricultural' as if it's a separate word.

I throw my chin in the air, refusing to bow to her no matter how much fear her words put in me. "That's not true, Lilith. The Test determines who qualifies for what job. I've been studying for this occupation for two years."

She rolls her eyes. "We'll see."

"Why?" I ask. "What occupation are you testing for?"

She smiles coldly, her eyes narrowing like a cat's. "Entertainment."

I'm not surprised, but I am through with the conversation. If I stand in the hallway arguing with Lilith all afternoon, I won't get to see Mom. "Goodbye, Lilith."

"Bye," she calls to me. "Just make sure you have a backup plan for when the original fails." She says it like she's reminding me to put on fresh underwear and wash behind my ears.

I don't bother with a wave as I head for the doors and Jamie beyond, but her words echo in my head. What if I don't get government? What other occupation could I get stuck with? Entertainment's out, since I'm not at all entertaining. I know how to grow things, thanks to Dad, but the thought of being in agriculture for the rest of my life sounds almost as bad as becoming a Lesser for not testing.

Jamie's long brown hair sways in a ponytail ahead of me. I'm glad for the distraction.

"Jamie!" I call out, waving over my head.

She turns around and sees me, then waits while I catch up.

Lilith is already forgotten. I lean toward Jamie and say, "Something strange happened yesterday."

3

"Something strange at the hospital?" she asks. This is why she's my best friend. She knows what I'm thinking even before I say it.

We walk the four blocks home together, just like we always do. She towers over me. We're as different in looks as night and day. I'm short, she's not. I have short blond hair, she has long brown hair. But inside? Kindred spirits.

"I overheard the doctors talking." My stomach rolls at the memory. "They said they were thinking about giving Mom chemo drugs." I glance around, remembering how it was supposed to be a secret. Not a single soul can be seen among the blooming trees on the quiet street.

Jamie's smooth face scrunches up. "Chemo drugs? I thought you said they didn't have those anymore."

I had explained all about the mutation and the treatment when Mom was first diagnosed. Jamie had held my hand and cried with me, and then listened as I explained every part of the mutation that I could understand enough to tell.

"Exactly." I round the corner onto our street. "That's why it's strange."

We stop in front of Jamie's house so she can put down her school bag. Jamie lives next door to me, but we always go to my house instead of hers after school. I have my own room, and she's always telling me how lucky I am for the privacy. I get what she's saying, but sometimes I wish my parents had opted to have both of the allowed two-children-per-family.

I breathe in the heady scent of the newly blooming trees as I wait for her, excited for summer to come. It's three weeks until graduation, and I'm ready for it.

"So, what do you think?" I say as we push through my unlocked front door.

Jamie shrugs and we head up the stairs. She kicks off her shoes and sits on my bed. "Maybe they're calling something else chemo drugs. Or maybe they've come up with a way to make the old ones again."

I bite my lip. "Maybe. The doctors were disagreeing about it, though. They said Mom would have to keep it secret. I guess I wasn't supposed to overhear them. They didn't see me listening." That part confuses me the most. Why shouldn't they help everyone, if they can? I thought that's what the Greaters were here for.

"Hana, they wouldn't keep secrets from your family. They're going to do all they can to help your mom." She squeezes me in a hug. "Do you want me to go with you to the hospital today?"

"That's OK," I say. I need to come to terms with this scary new life on my own. Besides, I'm not sure I agree with Jamie about the chemo drug issue. Maybe she's right, but I want to find out more before I forget about it completely. Like, if they're calling something else chemo, what is it? And if they can make the old drugs again, why aren't they telling people?

I want to ask her other things—like what she thinks about dying, and what happens afterward—but I don't. She was so quick to take the Greaters' side about the chemo; she'd probably just remind me about reincarnation, which is something I've never been too sure of no matter what the Greaters tell us.

"There was this medic in training there. He was really nice." I change the subject.

Jamie raises her eyebrows. "Have you already forgotten about Keegan? It's only been a couple of months since you saw him last."

Keegan is my other neighbor and is a year older than Jamie and I. He took his Test last year and has been away for training off and on ever since.

I let out a laugh, hoping my cheeks aren't turning red. I don't want her to know I thought the medic was cute and caring. "Not exactly, even though I think he's forgotten me. I haven't heard from him in at least two weeks. He never even responded to my letter about my mom's diagnosis." We have really great mail service these days. Letters can travel between cities by train within a couple of days. Our teachers tell us about something called email. They say it had traveled around the world in seconds, back in the Early Days. That would be so great.

"He probably just doesn't know what to say," she says. "If he was here he'd have the perfect words for you, but from far away he isn't sure. And he's busy training for his occupation. He'll write soon."

"I guess so," I say, but I'm not really sure of it. Why would he ignore my letter about Mom? We've been inseparable since we were little. I thought he'd be the first to comfort me when I wrote him a few weeks ago, and instead he's the one person I haven't heard from.

She gives me a stare down. "He'll write, Hana. He will."

I sigh and nod. "I know. It's only been two weeks.

And he's training for the future."

Jamie nods. "Exactly. A future with you."

"Besides, you'll be busy training too, after the Test. It's only three weeks away," she says in a sing-songy voice.

"Can you talk about something else to distract me?" I don't want to think about how little I've heard from Keegan any more.

Jamie smiles at me. Her eyes twinkle. "Of course."

I nod and we close our eyes. Meditation is a requirement, although it doesn't make me feel better. I really need the soothing affects after Mom's diagnosis, the questions about chemo drugs, and Keegan's silence on it all.

We breathe in and out. Deep, slow breaths, just like we've been taught.

"I've been seeing Easton," she says between breathing exercises. Easton goes to our school, and Jamie's been talking about changing her Test answers to reflect interest in agriculture, because that's what Easton wants to do. I told her it's crazy, and they're bound to get caught. My dad is the dean of the agriculture college, and while we don't always agree, he's not stupid. Our Tests determine what our optimal occupation is—or how we can best serve our small country. Faking on the Test is like letting the whole country down, and that is not a good thing. Besides, Jamie couldn't even grow a bean sprout for our third grade science project.

"What do you mean you've been seeing him?" I ask. "Like outside of school?"

"Yes."

I stop to stare at her. "Jamie, is that a good idea?"

"I think I love him."

"Jamie!" Hanging out alone with the opposite sex is against the law. It's the Greaters' form of birth control. "What do you do when you see each other?"

She gets back into position and closes her eyes. "Sometimes we meet at the levies. We just sit and talk and watch the river."

I study her for a minute, frowning, but then take her lead and go back to my meditation pose. "Don't do anything, you know, stupid."

She stays silent for so long I can't help looking at her.

"Jamie?"

She sighs and opens her eyes. "I won't, Hana. I promise."

I study her another moment, just to make sure she means it. We both shut our eyes and go back to meditation, but my mind wanders. I can picture them sitting on the levy, watching the murky water of what used to be the mighty Mississippi River, but now is more of a sluggish trickle.

We finish up and then study for an hour. After that, it's time to head to the hospital. I have to get there and back home before dark, because being out in the city after dark isn't allowed.

❧

The hospital lobby is empty and dim again, but I don't need the signs to find the stairs. The buzzing of the long bulbs on the third floor doesn't bother me as I pass the desk with the clunky computer. The young medic is sitting behind it. I pause.

He smiles when he recognizes me. "You're back!"

I smile and nod. "I'll probably be here a lot in the

next couple of weeks."

"Right. I'm sorry." He shakes his head.

"No, that's OK." I don't feel so stupid and nervous today. "I didn't get your name yesterday. If I'm going to be here so often, I would like to know everyone's name." I can't help it; it's my natural tendency to take control.

He grins. "I'm Fischer." He doesn't hold out his hand like the doctors did yesterday. Relief trickles through me, but so does a hint of disappointment.

"Nice to meet you. Officially." I stop and glance at the clunky machine on the desk. "What do you do with that thing?"

His eyebrows shoot up. "The computer? You've never used one?"

I shake my head.

He smiles again, and I suddenly wish I had fixed my hair instead of pulling it into a tight ponytail with half of it hanging out.

I immediately wince at the thought. I'm not one of those girls. I don't obsess about my looks, even though I try to look my best. Keegan's never made me feel anything but pretty, and I've always been confident in that. I take no extra pride in my hair or my body. Of course, my body isn't much different than anyone else's. I'm thin. Everyone is. The Greaters are supposedly always looking out for our health, and so we only get enough food allowance to keep us healthy. Back in the Early Days some people had a disease called obesity. The Greaters eliminated that disease. Too bad they can't do the same for the mutation.

Fischer doesn't seem to notice my discomfort. He pats the computer. "I'll show it to you one day when I don't have about a million other things to do."

"That would be great," I say with a smile.

"It's a deal then." He nods and goes back to his work.

I go on to Mom's room. She's awake and sitting up in bed today, and the lights are on. Relief surges through me because she looks good. Her hair is brushed smooth, and she's sipping a glass of dark liquid.

"Hi Hana," she says. "I heard I missed you yesterday."

I give her a light hug. I'm afraid to hug too tightly. "I stayed for a while, but I had to get home before dark."

She nods. "Of course. How's home?"

"It's fine. I've been cooking while you've been gone. At first Dad acted scared to try my fried squash, but he doesn't seem to mind now."

She laughs softly. "What about school?"

"Fine. Everyone's ready for the year to be out."

"Have you been doing the laundry?"

I roll my eyes. "Yes, Mom."

We talk for a while, and I hope she'll bring up her treatment. She doesn't. I want to know if they've mentioned the chemo, and then I can't wait anymore. "Mom, what are they going to do to help you?" My insides twist as I wait for her answer. *Please say chemotherapy.*

"They've been feeding me lots of strawberries and blueberries. Broccoli and tomatoes, too."

That ball is back in my throat. I swallow hard. "Is that it?"

"Well, besides the herbal tea of course." She nods toward the glass she's drinking from. "It's disgusting."

I laugh at her facial expression. Mom never has

liked tea. I got that from her, I guess. I glance toward the door to make sure no one is walking in, then I lean close. "They haven't said anything about medicines? I mean *real* medicines?"

My mom frowns and leans toward me. "What do you mean?"

"You know, like chemo drugs or something."

She chuckles and leans back. "I wish. Someday we may get back to that success level as a society, but we aren't there yet."

That's what you think, I want to say. But then another thought hits me. Maybe she's keeping it a secret, just like Dr. Bentford said she would have to.

That has to be it. My mom served in our small country's military—what she was protecting us from I don't know—and she is great at all things soldierish, including secret keeping. The thought gives me a sliver of hope, and I sit back and enjoy the rest of my visit.

4

"Are you sure you don't want me to come to the hospital with you?" Jamie asks the next day after school. "I really don't mind."

I shake my head. I don't know how to describe it to her, but I want all of Mom's time to myself. I miss her being at home with me, and I want to be the center of her attention when I actually get to be with her. It's only been a few days since she was put in the hospital, but it feels like forever without her at home.

Jamie bites her lip. "If you're sure."

I wonder what she's going to do if she doesn't come to the hospital. Easton's face pops in my mind and I cringe, wondering if she'll be meeting him instead.

The door to my house bangs open and Dad sprints across the threadbare yard. For some reason, grass has never grown well there, and not being able to grow something has been a thorn in his side for years. "Hana! I forgot to give this to you. I picked it up at the post office today."

I don't want to let myself hope, but I glance down at the letter. *Keegan!*

"Thanks, Dad." I smile at him, trying to seem like it's no big deal, but I can tell I'm not pulling it off.

He nods and waves, then goes back inside. He knows I'm heading to the hospital. We take turns visiting at night, but mostly he goes during the daytime, on his lunch break.

Jamie watches me expectantly.

I hold up the letter for her to see.

She looks at the name on the envelope and smiles. "See?"

I smile back and shrug. "I know."

"Tell me what it says after you read it."

"I will." I head toward the side walk. The letter burns a hole in my pocket as I walk the blocks to the hospital. I could read it in a hurry before I go up to Mom's room, but I want to savor it. I'll wait until I get home.

A handful of people congregate in the lobby of the hospital today. I might have been surprised, but I know they're here for Markus Huckleberry. His twin sister told everyone at school today that he'd fallen out of a tree last night and got a concussion.

She spots me and jogs over. "What are you doing here, Hana?"

"Hey, Ava. I'm visiting my mom. How's Markus?"

Ava pauses like she isn't sure what to say. "He's OK, I guess. We haven't got to see him yet. I forgot about your mom. I'm sorry."

I shrug. "It's OK. I'll see you around, OK?" Ava's nice. She and Markus are a grade behind me in school, but when we've been together in the past, they've always been great. Her family has a lot of money because they own more than one business in our city, but she doesn't act like there's any difference between her and the poorest Middles. My dad says that Ava's dad used to be Greater, but when he took his Test at seventeen, he scored as a Middle. Still, I guess everything he learned in Greater City stuck, because he's very successful here.

What she said sticks in my mind, though. They haven't got to see him? If he was brought in last night then why wouldn't they be able to see him this afternoon?

Fischer isn't at his desk today, and as usual, the hall is deserted. A short stack of folders sits on the desk beside the computer. I'm not looking on purpose, but I spot Mom's name on an open folder. I saw the doctors writing in her file that first day. What did they say in there? I can't help it, I have to know. I glance around to make sure I'm still alone, and with a pounding pulse I flip open the file.

Chemotherapy drugs: requested.

Tears burn my eyes so fast I'm embarrassed. They did it! They're going to give Mom chemotherapy. It feels strange to be happy about poison. I've even heard some people argue against redeveloping the chemo drugs, saying they're harmful. Those people have obviously never had a mom with the mutation.

Hot tears run down my cheeks and I swipe them away. Now my eyes are going to be puffy and Mom is going to ask me what's wrong. I hate it when people see me cry.

Then another thought hits me. It's Fischer's job to go through the folders. I saw him doing something with them yesterday, when he was messing with the computer.

So he knows about chemo drugs. What else does he know about? Markus Huckleberry?

I suddenly want to get to know Fischer better. I want to know what he knows. I want to know as soon as the chemo drugs are approved.

Fischer walks down the hall, back toward his desk. He smiles when he spots me.

Katie Clark

"Hi Hana. How are you today?"

I shrug. "I'm OK." I hope it's not obvious I was crying, and I glance at the stack of folders to make sure my spying isn't noticeable.

His eyes show concern. I guess it *is* obvious I was crying. "Anything I can do to help?"

Yes! I want to shout. Instead, I shake my head. "No, but, if I needed you, um, later, could I talk to you then?"

"Absolutely. Just let me know, OK?"

"Sure. Thank you, Fischer."

He smiles now. "You're welcome."

I'm about to turn away, but I pause. "You're not from our city are you?" I'm not sure why I ask. Maybe because he acts so nice, or maybe because I'm trying to get to know him.

His smile stretches a little further across his face. "How did you know?"

I'm too embarrassed to admit I think he's nice. "You talk funny."

"I'm from a city further south. It used to be called Paducah, Kentucky."

My geography lessons from school flash through my mind, and I know that Paducah isn't that far from our own city. Of course, most cities aren't that far from our city. Our civilization only covers a small area. Back in the Early Days, the environment kept getting more volatile. Hurricanes, tornadoes, and earthquakes happened constantly, and coast lines and states were wiped out. Once the country was so weak, enemies from across the oceans attacked. Entire generations were lost, and the survivors moved as far inland as they could. They formed what is now our country about two hundred years ago.

"Are you here for your training?" I ask. It's a stupid question, since the answer is obvious. Our city houses the training facilities for medical, agriculture, and military.

He nods. "Yep, third year medic. Have you taken your Test yet?"

I shake my head. "I graduate in three weeks."

"You'll do great, I'm sure. Do you know what occupation you hope to get?"

"I want to work in government," I say. I don't know why I tell him, considering the reaction I got in school the other day. Maybe because I can tell he won't laugh at me.

I'm right.

"That's great. Is there a particular reason?"

"I want to help the Lessers. It feels like we should be able to do more for them. There has to be a better way for them to live." I remember the mental picture I've carried of the skeletal boy from Mom's story.

He stares at me so long I start to get nervous. His eyes aren't confused or judgmental like Lilith's were. They almost seem—awed. Finally, he smiles. "Don't worry. Like I said, I'm sure you'll do great."

He gets to work, and I go to Mom's room.

After I'm in her room—she's sleeping again—I realize that Fischer made me forget all about Keegan's letter.

After an hour I'm fighting my own sleepiness, but I can't bring myself to leave. I want to talk to Mom so bad I consider just waking her up. A knock raps at the door, and Dr. Lane comes in.

"Hi Hana. How are you?"

"I'm fine. A little bored, but fine."

She smiles. "Patients with the mutation do sleep a

lot, especially your mom's type. The mutation is in the blood, and it makes her more tired than you can imagine."

I like Dr. Lane, especially since she was the one who wanted to give Mom chemo drugs, but mostly because she seems genuinely interested in me. I almost want to ask her about the chemo, but I keep my mouth shut. She might be upset if she found out I had heard her, and after that she might not be so open and kind.

I stay too late hoping Mom will wake up, but she doesn't. Twilight has set in by the time I'm outside. My legs burn because I walk so fast. Only a few people dot the streets and most of them seem to be in front of their own homes. What will happen if I get caught after dark? Curfew is strictly enforced. I've never cut it so close, and my heart beats faster with each step.

The sun disappears behind the horizon just as I turn onto my street. I'm practically jogging by now. When I make it to my house I push through my front door and slam it behind me.

"What kept you so late?" Dad asks, looking up. He had been bent over his work, and I doubt he even realizes I broke the city curfew.

"Mom was sleeping, and I tried to wait for her to wake up." I don't mention I was there for hours—he already knows it.

He nods nonchalantly, but I can tell he's trying not to cry. He misses Mom, and he's scared like I am. Scared she might not live. Scared of what that will mean for all of us.

I stand at the steps going upstairs to my room, unsure if I should hug him or ask what he thinks will happen to Mom. We love each other, but we don't have the open relationship Mom and I have. "I'll start on supper in a minute, OK?" Keegan's letter is begging to be read.

He waves me off. "I'm working on lessons for tomorrow. Take your time."

I take the stairs two at a time to my room and rip open the letter. I drink in his handwriting like cold water on a hot day.

Dear Hana, I'm sorry it's taken me so long to write back. I'm sorry about your mom. It really, really isn't fair. We can talk about it soon, because I'll be home on break in a couple of weeks.

You wouldn't believe this city! It's twice the size of ours, and there are Greaters swarming the place, even though it's a Middle city. Working in the entertainment industry is very awesome. I've met two singers and a handful of actors. Some of them even guest lecture at my school. I can't believe it's already been a year since my Test, and I can't wait until you pass yours. I know you'll get government, Hana. Then we'll be together again. I have so much to tell you when I get home. I can't wait to see you. Until then, Keegan.

I stare at the letter, flipping it front to back. I grab the envelope and look in it again. There's got to be more. But the envelope is empty. Hot disappointment seeps through my bones. It spreads from my heart into each of my limbs.

I bite my lip. At least he wrote. That's all that matters. I try not to feel upset at the short note. I try and fail.

Katie Clark

5

Tables line the gymnasium of our hundred-year-old school. Representatives from each of the occupational universities sit behind the tables— military, agriculture, medical, entertainment, teaching, business, government, law enforcement, and science.

A small sea of kids wanders through the gym, talking to different representatives and asking questions.

I stand back, clipboard in hand, watching the progress of the career fair. Pride surges through me as I watch successful interviews and happy faces.

"You did well." Mrs. Sewell stands beside me, smiling.

"Thank you." I arranged for the university reps to come, got the gymnasium set up, and worked out a schedule for students who were graduating with me this year. Each graduate is provided an education allowance that pays for their college. While the Test determines what occupation we get, we are encouraged to try for the one we want the most. This way everyone has a better chance of being happy with their lives.

Lilith's words come back to me, taunting me. What will I do if I don't get to work in government? What if I don't have aptitude for that type of work after all?

"Aren't you going to talk to the government representative?" Mrs. Sewell asks, almost as if she can hear my thoughts.

My cheeks heat up. "Actually, I asked him to have lunch with me."

She grins. "That's the way to take initiative, Hana. Nice work." She moves into the gym to mingle with the other students, and I step back to make sure things run smoothly.

"Can I ask you a question?" someone says.

I turn to find Graham, a fellow graduate. "Sure, what do you need?"

He glances around, biting his lip. "I really like experimenting, and I'd like to help people who are sick, but I don't know if that's science or medical."

"Science, definitely."

"Thanks, Hana." He scurries away.

I sigh and lean back against the wall. Mrs. Sewell says this type of experience would be good for my work in the government, especially when it comes to putting programs together to help the Lessers. They are violent people, lazy people, and unproductive people. I can't help but think our country would be better if someone stepped in to help them, even if I haven't figured out how that might happen.

A door opens to my right, and I turn my head. Jamie slips outside.

I frown, trying to remember if I saw her talking with any of the reps. I don't want to worry, but I can't help but glance around for Easton.

He's there, talking to a rep from agriculture. I'm glad, but where is she going?

I scan the crowd, looking for other familiar faces. True to her word, Lilith stands at the entertainment table. The representative watches her raptly, and I hope Lilith isn't going to break out in song to prove her skill. I can just imagine her doing that to impress someone.

Only a handful of kids even bother with the government rep. He sighs and lets out a yawn. That doesn't surprise me, of course. Especially if everyone believes like Lilith that you need special connections to get a government job.

The door to my right clicks closed again and I turn. Easton is gone. I frown and consider going after them. What are they up to? I strain to see them out the window next to the door, but they're gone.

I want to follow them, but I can't. I'm in charge of this event. Taking a deep breath, I force myself to stay put.

We finish up career day in the gym, and after I help clean up I meet the government rep in the cafeteria. He's sitting casually at a table, some type of portfolio spread out in front of him.

"Hi, Mr. Sims," I say, sliding into the seat across from him. "It was so nice of you to meet with me like this."

He smiles, his white teeth sparkling in the sunlight that comes through the windows. He's only a few years older than me, and I'm more convinced than ever that I don't need any special connections for a job alongside him.

"It's a pleasure," he says. "I like to see young people who are excited about the running of our country and who take steps to reinforce our values and systems."

"Exactly!" I say. "I definitely want to make our country as good as it can be."

We talk about programs that are currently in place for the Lessers, as well as allowances and spending habits in the Lesser cities. He seems excited about my ideas, and I'm definitely excited about the classes we discuss. The time flies.

"Lunch hour's up!" someone calls from the cafeteria door.

Mr. Sims stands and holds out his hand, just like the doctors did at the hospital.

I take it, reluctantly.

"It was great talking with you, Hana. I'm sure you're going to pass your Test with flying colors."

"Thank you again, Mr. Sims," I say with a smile.

The students shuffle out to find their classes. Jamie is ahead of me, heading into English class. I had forgotten about her absence during the career fair, and I was too busy during lunch to think about it. I want to ask her what's up as I slide into the desk beside hers, but I can't bring myself to do it. I don't have any proof that she's doing something dangerous or wrong.

After school we walk home together. Her disappearing act has played in my mind a dozen times. "Did you talk to any reps today?" I ask, trying to break the ice.

"Sure," she says with a shrug. "I talked to someone from agriculture and someone else from business."

"Business? That would be great!" I'm glad to hear she talked to someone besides agriculture. It shows she hasn't given up on her own dreams after all. It's not that I'm against her and Easton being together, but the thought of her getting caught doing something illegal twists my stomach in knots. *Demotion* is a scary word.

She shrugs again. "I guess so. My mom and dad said they would help me open a grocery store if I wanted to. I saw you talking to the government official at lunch. How did it go?"

Now it's my turn to shrug. "It went really well. I can't believe the Test is so close."

She smiles. "Me, either."

She's acting normal, not like she's done anything to break a rule—or a law. Maybe I'm being paranoid.

"I saw Lilith Winters talking to the entertainment rep," Jamie says. "I was afraid she was going to start singing right then and there."

"Me too!" I say. We start laughing then, just like always. "I thought for sure she would do her best to impress us all. She probably thought they'd make her Greater right off the bat."

Jamie nods. "The hottest new thing!"

We giggle some more, and I'm convinced there's nothing wrong with Jamie. Things are fine, and nothing is going on. Everything is great.

6

It starts raining just as we get home from school, and it's not just a light drizzle. Thunder crackles in the sky, and the rain comes down in sheets. After Jamie goes home, Dad says he wants to go see Mom this afternoon, even though he went earlier. He wants to be with her, he says. He tells me to stay home and stay dry. I find that hard to do. The house is too quiet without anyone else there, and I still haven't got Jamie and Easton's escapade out of my mind.

I peek out my window into Jamie's room across our small alley. The houses on our street are lined up one after the other, packed in like books on a shelf. I can see straight into her room. When we were little we used to play games tossing things across to see if it would make it into the next window. Once, we tossed an egg Mom had bought at the food market. It didn't make it across, which wouldn't have been so bad except Jamie's dad was in the alley, and the egg splattered on his bald head. I don't remember playing the game much after that.

Jamie's room looks empty. The curtains are open, and I don't see anyone inside, not even her little sister. I glance to her living room windows, and they're all dark. We don't typically use lamps during the day, but it's dark because of the rain clouds, so I'd expect some lights to be on.

All of our allowances are based on a per person

ratio. Each family's house has a meter, and the meters are set to allow a certain amount of electricity. Once that allowance is reached, no extra electricity will flow into the house until the next cycle at the start of a new month. The same goes for gas and water, so maybe her family is just out of their allowance.

"This is ridiculous," I mutter. I decide to just knock on her front door. I pull on my rain jacket and boots, and slosh through the rain.

No one answers the door. Jamie just left my house a half hour ago. Where could she be? That piques my interest, and since I'm already in my coat and boots I decide to do a little spy work in the rain.

I know a covered path to the levy that I can get to across the street. It's well-worn from years of kids playing and people fishing at the river, and it's shielded by trees. I should be able to keep dry, for the most part.

Water pelts my rubber arms, and my hands start to tingle with cold by the end of the twenty minute walk. I haven't seen another person, or any sign of anyone walking in the mud. When I come out of the trees, something catches my eye. The path is beat down more than normal. Tree branches are broken, and most of the grass in the area is matted down. It looks like a wrestling match took place in the trees.

I sneak forward, hoping my brown coat will camouflage me in the tree bark. I don't see anyone. I climb a little further up the hill, my legs shivering and slipping in the cold rain. The river is on the other side of the levy, and they might be sitting on that side, though why anyone would come to the river during a rain storm is beyond me. Maybe there were a few holes in my reason for coming.

Regardless, no one is on that side, either. Jamie's probably at home, safe and dry and asleep in her living room. I can't believe I did this.

I tromp back down the levy and toward the path. Lightning flashes in the sky and I hurry toward the trees, waiting for the thunder. It doesn't come. Strange. I glance to the sky one last time, and the flashing light is still there.

Even stranger.

The odd red and white lights dance and blink. It's definitely not lightning, so what is it? It's away from the city, not toward it, and people in their homes probably won't see the lights that far away. I wouldn't have seen them either, except I'd trudged out here hoping to spy on my best friend.

The blinking finally stops. How long have I been standing there? The sky is less light then it was before, and I hope I can get home before Dad does, not to mention curfew. No one caught me yesterday when I probably could have gotten by with a warning. Tonight though, I have no legitimate excuse for being out. What are those lights in the sky, though? A creepy tingling burns all over my body, and I hurry through the trees, dodging branches and soggy falling leaves. I make it home just in time.

The light is on in Jamie's room as I strip from my dripping clothes. She glances over and waves. I wave back.

"Where were you?" I ask. We've gotten pretty good at lip reading over the years.

"Downstairs," she says. "You?"

I shrug. "Out."

She waves again and I finish getting undressed. She thinks I was at the hospital, which is good because

I don't want her suspecting I was out looking for her. Guilt wedges its way into my head. How could I spy on my best friend?

But the guilt is replaced by a bigger worry. I can't get the flashing light out of my mind. What on earth could rise into the sky so high and blink like that, even in the pouring rain? It reminds me of stories from the Early Days, when enemy countries used their flying machines to devastate our land. What if the enemy is returning? I can't help wonder if I should report it, but to whom?

The guards are the law enforcement of our city, but we all know they don't have any real authority. They issue citations for those who break minor laws, like breaking curfew or being caught trading allowances. They report to the government officials, who take care of any more serious infractions. The government officials report directly to Frost Moon, our country's Great Supreme. I'm not sure who in that line would be appropriate to tell, not that I have any access to the Great Supreme anyway.

I pull on my pajamas and shiver. I didn't realize how cold I was.

Whatever the lights were, I hope I never have to cross them again. They give me an anxious feeling.

I cook vegetable soup for supper. Vegetables are a staple in our house, since we have a garden in our backyard. The gardens aren't required, but if you have them you get extra allowances to make up for the food allowance you don't need. Besides, Dad insists on it since he works for the agricultural university. He says he can't teach it if he's not living it. The soup's ready when Dad comes in.

"How was Mom?" I ask.

He sighs. "She looks good. She says she feels like the treatments are working. Dr. Bentford was there, and he explained that the order in which they give the nutrients affects the mutations. It was a lot to take in."

I give Dad an awkward hug. "She's going to be OK." I don't mention how I know it to him, but the words from her file run through my mind as if they've been imprinted in my brain: *chemotherapy: requested.*

He smiles, even though his eyes tell me he doesn't mean it. "How was your afternoon?"

I give back the same expression. "Uninteresting."

7

"Hana, wait!" Ava calls after school a few days later. Jamie and I walk out of the school doors, but we stop. Ava and I haven't spoken since that day in the hospital lobby. Why does she want to talk to me now?

I turn, and Ava almost runs into me.

"Sorry," she says, tucking her short black curls behind her ear.

I laugh. "It's OK. How's Markus?"

Her face clouds over. "Actually that's what I wanted to talk to you about. Are you going to see your mom at the hospital today?"

"Yeah, sure," I say. "We were going to do meditation first, though."

Ava glances at Jamie. "Do you mind if I tag along?"

The request surprises me. Ava's nice, and we've known each other our whole lives, but we've never been what one would call friends.

"It's OK with me," I say. "What do you think, Jamie?"

Jamie shrugs. "No problem." But her eyes dart away, and I wonder if it actually is a problem. Jamie's been acting strange today. I almost wish Ava wasn't coming. Then maybe I could try talking to Jamie again.

We walk the four blocks home, the sun glaring down on us. It's finally chased away the rain from yesterday. I look toward the eastern sky, where I saw the lights the night before. Nothing's there but blue sky and white clouds. I haven't mentioned the lights to anyone. I'd have to explain being out at the levies by myself. In the rain.

We don't talk during the walk, but the silence isn't awkward. One after the other we head upstairs to my room.

"Do you have a meditation mat?" I ask when we get to my room. Some people meditate more than others, and they carry their mats in backpacks. "You can borrow one of my parent's if not."

"I don't have one," Ava says.

I smile. "That's fine. I'll be right back."

I return with Mom's black mat and we roll them out in a line of three across my floor. It's a tight fit, but I don't mind. It feels cozy. Comfortable. Safe.

I work to clear my mind. No thoughts of cancer. No thoughts of Keegan's brief letter. No thoughts of flashing lights in the sky or Jamie's odd behavior.

I am a seagull drifting over the calm, quiet ocean.

I am an eagle soaring over majestic mountain tops.

I am a cheetah running scared through the trees.

I snap out of my peacefulness and glance at Ava and Jamie. They still have their eyes closed. I close mine again, but I can't meditate anymore. I know that last image is truer than the first two. My life has become more scary and confusing, and less peaceful and calm.

We finish and roll up our mats. I wave to Jamie as Ava and I split from her in front of her house. "I'll see you later."

"Bye guys," she says. "See you around."

Ava smiles but doesn't say anything. At first we walk in silence, and I wonder why she asked to come with me in the first place. Step. Step. Step. Step. The lack of talking starts to feel strange.

"So, Markus is still in the hospital?" I ask.

She frowns and nods, but keeps walking silently.

"When will he get out?"

"I don't know. I keep hearing my parents whispering about it, but no one talks to me about anything."

That explains why she's so out of sorts. Secrets are never good things, and I wonder exactly what's going on with Markus. "What floor is he on?"

"The second floor. We haven't even seen him since the accident."

"Really?" That's definitely odd.

"No one will let us in. That bothers me as much as my parents' whisperings." She hugs herself, never looking at me.

"I'm sorry, Ava. That sounds really awful." And it does. At least I have an idea what's going on in Mom's body. Ava doesn't have any reassurances or hopes. She doesn't really know if he's even alive.

"Do you want to come with me to visit my mom? Then I can go with you to Markus' room. Maybe they'll let you in today."

She stops and stares at me. "Really? You wouldn't mind if I came with you?"

"Of course not." I know why she thinks my kindness is so strange. Most people really aren't that nice. Fischer must have rubbed off on me a tiny bit, or maybe it's just that when you've been through something pretty awful you want to help other people who feel awful, too.

In the hospital, we climb the concrete stairs in silence, and the heavy metal door clanks shut behind us as we enter the third floor.

"Hi Hana," Fischer says. He glances up from his stack of folders and stops what he's doing when he sees Ava. "Hi there."

Ava smiles and gives him a small wave. "Hi."

I glance back and forth between them. Does Fischer know Ava? "This is my friend Ava. Her brother is on the second floor. He fell out of a tree."

Fischer frowns, but only for a second. "I'm sorry to hear that. I'm Fischer." He doesn't hold out his hand to shake Ava's hand, and I'm glad. I had wondered if there was a reason he didn't shake my hand after the doctors had done it. Obviously, he just doesn't shake.

"We're going to visit my mom," I say. "Is it OK to have more than one guest?" I don't know why I didn't think of that before, but Fischer nods immediately.

"Absolutely. Go ahead."

He smiles at Ava again, and we walk down the hall.

My mom is awake today. She has an extra big smile for Ava. "Who's this?"

"I'm Ava," she says. "I came with Hana. I hope you don't mind."

"I don't mind at all!" Mom says. "I'm so tired of these walls, and seeing the same four people every day. Not you, Hana, the medics and doctors. Thank you for coming, Ava."

I tell Mom who Ava's family is, and why she's here.

My mom frowns. "I know your mom. We were friends a long time ago. I'm sorry about your brother. I hope he's OK."

Ava smiles. "Thank you."

We talk and laugh for about an hour. Ava turns

out to be even nicer than I knew. She wants to help
Mom in any way she can and is always adjusting her
pillows or getting her more water. I ask her if she's
going to try and test for a medic.

She blushes. "I don't know. I guess I'll just see
what the Test shows."

A lot of kids do that. They don't really know what
they want to do, and it's not like there are that many
choices.

"You'd make a really good nurse," I say.

We finish visiting with Mom and then head to the
second floor. Medics rush through the hall, and
families lounge outside of rooms. "This floor is so
busy," I say.

"I think they keep people with injuries and
sicknesses on this floor," she says. "You know, things
like broken bones or pneumonia." Sicknesses are
common since we don't have many medicines.

"His room's this way," she says. We go to the right
and come to a closed door. Ava knocks and tries the
knob, but it's locked. "Same as yesterday."

After a moment a medic opens the door from the
inside. We can just see her face through the crack she's
opened up. "Can I help you?"

"I'm here to see Markus. I'm his sister."

The medic shakes her head. "You can't see him.
I'm sorry." She begins to close the door.

"Please, just for a moment," Ava says.

"I have orders to let no one in. You'll have to
leave."

Ava's bottom lip quivers and her eyes become
glossy.

My gaze darts back and forth between Ava and
the retreating medic. This is just so strange, and with

the chemotherapy and flashing lights in the sky, Ava
not being able to see her brother for no reason is too
much. "Wait!" I say.

The medic freezes.

I can't believe she's giving me a chance, but I don't
want to blow it so I step forward. "How is he? Can't
you at least tell us what's going on? Is he even alive?"

Ava cries harder.

The medic glances between the two of us. She bites
her lip and shakes her head. "I'm sorry. I'm not
allowed to say anything." She shuts the door.

Ava covers her face with her hands, and I offer a
hug. It's strange to hold her this way, but it seems to
help. Her crying quiets some.

"I'm sorry," she says. "I'm so worried about him,
and I keep imagining all the horrible things that might
be wrong with him. And you're right, is he even alive
in there?"

I swallow hard, not sure what to say. "Do you
want me to walk you home?" I finally ask.

She sniffs. "You don't mind?"

How could I? "No. It's no problem."

It's already twilight when we leave the hospital,
and I just hope I get home before dark.

8

The sun sets a few minutes after I leave Ava at her doorstep, and while she only lives a few blocks from me, there isn't time to make it to my yard before a guard stops me.

"Do you have ID?" she asks me. She towers over me, and her dull, brown hair is pulled into a ponytail at her neck. She wears standard issue police gear—a brown shirt and pants, with a police insignia sewn on the shirt pocket.

"No ma'am. I just came from visiting my mom in the hospital." I can hear my blood pumping in my ears. What will she do to me?

"Where do you live?"

"Three houses up. My name is Hana Norfolk." I look longingly at the dirty white house I call home. What if she takes me to the guard station and Dad has to come pick me up? If I have a mark on my record will it hurt my chances of getting into the government occupation I want? Surely they don't demote you on your first infringement.

The guard punches a few buttons into a small machine she carries. I've never seen anything like that before. Of course, I haven't been stopped by any guards before, either. "Daughter of Miles and Maya Norfolk?"

"Yes, ma'am," I say.

"This is the first time you've been out after

curfew?"

That I've been caught? "Yes."

The guard nods tersely. "I'm going to let you go this time, but I won't be so nice if I catch you again. We'll be watching, Hana. Don't let it happen again. Strange things can happen in the dark."

No kidding. I nod and smile apologetically. "Yes, ma'am. It won't happen again." I can't keep the relief from my voice.

Her authoritative face transforms into a smile, and she punches a few more buttons. "OK, you're free to go."

I hurry the few steps to my house and step inside. My dad is pacing the floor.

I bite my lip, afraid of what he'll say.

"What happened, Hana?"

"Sorry Dad, I—"

"You're sorry? You could have been attacked or caught by a guard. You know the laws, Hana. Would you like to tell me what you were doing?" His voice rises with each sentence.

I grit my teeth together, trying not to say something stupid. I do know the laws of the city. Don't break curfew. Stay within your allowances. Meditate every day. I've barely broken any of my parents' rules in my life, let alone broken a law. It's not fair for him to yell at me the first time I get in trouble. I take a deep breath and make myself talk in a calm voice. "I walked a friend home from the hospital. She was pretty upset because her twin brother is in the hospital and they won't let her see him."

My dad seems surprised by this. "Really?" But then his scowl is back. "You didn't get stopped, did you?"

"Actually, a guard stopped me. She let me go, though. She said not to let it happen again."

A worry line forms on Dad's forehead, but he finally nods. "OK." He leans against the couch and sighs. "No harm done."

I'm not sure what he means by that. What would happen if it *did* happen again? What would happen if there was harm done?

I race upstairs to take off my shoes, and my mind goes back to the guard. What was the machine she carried? How did she know who my parents were? I know in the Early Days they had all kinds of crazy technology, but all that was lost. Wasn't it? Why would it be kept from us if it was still around?

But maybe it isn't kept from us. She had it in the open, didn't she?

I press the heels of my hands into my eyes. This is so confusing.

After supper I dig through my stuff to find my ID. The next time I'm asked for it, I want to have it available. I find it in an old backpack and stare at it. The girl in the picture seems foreign to me. This ID was made when I turned thirteen. I will be issued a new one after I take my Test and am assigned a status. I slide it into my pocket.

My gaze goes to Jamie's window by habit. Her room is dark. She must be in the living room with her family. I suddenly want to test the limits of this city. I want to find out how far I can go.

Hidden chemo drugs? Denied access to hospital visits? Foreign blinking lights in the sky? Something feels off. I look out the window toward Middle City 3, and I wonder if I'll ever know what it is.

What would happen if I went out the back door

and visited Jamie in her living room? Would her family even let me in? What could be so wrong with trotting across the yard? Surely no one lurks in my vegetable garden.

Of course, there is always the danger of a Lesser on the loose. They mostly stay in their own communities, but sometimes they sneak past the guards and end up in our city, or even Greater City. They always commit crimes when they're on the loose. Thefts, vandals, even murders. This is why we're supposed to stay in after curfew.

But after the strange blinking lights, I'm not sure I fully believe it. What if the Lessers aren't the only reason we have a curfew?

So the question begs asking, if the Lessers aren't the reason, what is?

I try to go to bed then, but my mind is restless. I have too many questions and no answers. Too many problems and no solution. I'm a natural problem solver, and it kills me that I can't solve these issues.

I glance again at Jamie's house. I won't go, of course, but I would like to.

9

Graduation is two weeks away. Mrs. Sewell asks me to help my classmates prepare their paperwork for their Tests before our Sunday break. I finish up with Graham Miller, and then step to the next student. I stifle a groan because it's Lilith Winters. She's dazzling in a crisp white dress against her coal-black hair. How did she manage to get a dress like that, since no one has enough allowance for some things? Regardless, she'll make a stunning entertainer dressed like that.

"I don't really need any help," she says. Her bright blue eyes dance icily.

If it wasn't about ninety degrees in the school I would probably shiver.

"Do you have your essay written?"

She nods. "Of course."

I don't know why I bother helping her. I should probably let her mess up—but of course I won't. I have to do the right thing. "And you've filled out the front and back of the questionnaire?"

She pauses. "Yes."

My eyes narrow. "Are you sure you don't want any help?"

"Nope, I've got it under control."

I shrug and slide to the next student, but I see Lilith pull her questionnaire from her folder. I'd bet my entertainment allowance she didn't look at the back.

"Can you help me word part of my essay?"

Bernadette asks.

"No problem. Which part?" I slide into the desk beside her. Bernadette's quiet, but when she speaks, people listen. I'm eager to see what she has to say on paper.

She points to her essay, and I scan while she talks. "I can't word exactly how I feel about the Greaters, and how they provide for us all. I want to express how I want to teach that to future generations."

The Greaters have met my every need, including food, education, and entertainment. They've given me a place to live and provided laws to keep my family safe and happy. It is my hope to relay the knowledge of these blessings to future generations of our society. This is why I want to be a teacher. I want to train the future generations to make our society brighter.

I stare at the paper, hearing Bernadette but not hearing at all. How can I help her express how good the Greaters are when I'm not sure I believe it anymore? Are the Greaters good? And other problems with her logic pop out at me. A place to live? The houses and buildings were in our city long before the Greaters established a new nation, and the laws that keep us safe and happy are also working to keep us quiet and ignorant.

"What do you think?" Bernadette asks when I don't say anything.

I sit back with a sigh. "I think what you've written comes off right, but let me think about it, OK?"

She accepts this answer without comment, and I hurry to Mrs. Sewell. "I need to use the restroom, Mrs. Sewell." I've got to clear my head.

She waves me away, and I hurry to the hall. The hallway is empty, besides two boys who walk toward me. The bigger one has his arm around the smaller one. Neither is in the graduating class, and I'm not sure of their names, but the bigger one looks familiar. I smile and wave.

The bigger one smirks at me and the other keeps his head down, almost like he's cowering away from the first boy.

I frown as they pass, and when I reach the restroom I turn around to see where they've gone. I catch a glimpse of the first one holding the second one against the wall. He shoves the boy against a locker and mutters something close to his face.

The smaller boy nods quickly, obviously agreeing with whatever the bigger boy is saying. Still, the smaller boy's feet begin to lift off the ground.

I remember the older boy's name then, it's Kohen Lamb. He's been suspended from school once already for kicking a boy in the bathroom. The boy ended up with a broken rib.

Just then Kohen turns to me. He sees me standing there, witnessing his fury. Apparently, he doesn't like it because he drops the little boy and heads toward me. The boy lets out an *oomph* when he hits the floor, and he curls into a ball.

My heart speeds into double time and my brain screams *think fast!* I can't go into the bathroom. He'll just follow me. Instead, I sprint down the hall, toward the principal's office. I can hear him behind me at first, but then the sound fades. I don't slow down. I arrive out of breath and panting. The rubber band that held my hair in a ponytail snapped while I ran, and now my hair hangs in my face. I push into the principal's office. He takes one look at me and jumps from his seat.

"What is it, Hana?" he asks, frowning.

"Kohen Lamb is chasing me. He's in the hall. He was beating up some little kid."

The principal follows me back to the hall, but Kohen is gone. The principal helps the younger boy get cleaned up and sends me back to class.

I still haven't gone to the bathroom, so I slip into a stall while I will my nerves to calm down. I splash cool water on my face and take a deep breath. After a few minutes pass, I stick my head out the door. The principal has Kohen cornered. I hear words like "third strike" and "Lesser." I shudder as I think about the bully being sent to a Lesser city, and I'm reminded of why our government system works. Those who bully others, who hurt them, who are violent and unruly, should be sent away. That is who the Lessers are. Our government knows this. They know it well, and that's why the rules are in place.

Jamie comes to mind then, and I remember how she's been meeting Easton outside of school. Alone. She's breaking the law, too.

I shake my head. Jamie's OK. She's not doing anything stupid, so even if she gets caught alone with Easton she won't be sent away.

I creep from the restroom and return to class. My adrenaline still pumps, but I think I'm prepared to help Bernadette now.

10

School is out on Sundays. It's the only free day each week, and I want to spend this morning with Mom. After my visit, I'll meet up with Jamie so we can go to the market together. Our food allowances go from Monday through Sunday, and we need to use what we have left before they expire.

Mom is sleeping when I get to the hospital. Dark circles line her eyes, even in her sleep, and her breaths are shallow and quick. I swallow hard. What happens if the natural treatments don't work? My mom has always been there for me, no matter what. She was the first person who ever suggested I would like working in government. I like solving problems; making things better. I'm good at it, and can work through problems logistically and objectively. She never pushes me to be the person she wants, only to be the best person I can be. She listens when I talk and offers advice.

Just the thought of her absence makes my stomach clench. I can't imagine living in the house with only Dad. It doesn't mean I don't love him; it's just that he's always busy working on lessons or growing super veggies. And he's not Mom.

My mind drifts to the folders that are usually stacked on Fischer's desk. How long does it take to get approval for the chemo drugs? It's been a week now, plenty of time for a message to get back and forth between cities.

Before I know it, I'm in the hallway. Fischer isn't around that I can see, and I inch toward his workspace. The folders are there, but Mom's isn't on top. I lay my arm casually on the counter and glance around. I'm still alone. I hope I look casual on the outside, because on the inside I think even my bones are shaking.

I slide one folder a couple of inches, then another folder, and another. The fourth folder down is marked "Maya Norfolk."

"Do you need something?"

Fischer's voice spins me around like a whirlwind. Words don't come, but tears do.

He looks nervous himself, and he keeps glancing between Mom's folder and me. "I have a break in about ten minutes. I like to eat on the roof. Would you like to join me?"

What's he talking about? I shake my head. "I can't. I—"

"I really hope you will, Hana." He closes Mom's file and takes the stack away.

I watch him go, my heart hammering. Is he going to report me? Why does he want to talk to me? The last thing I want to do now is meet with him on the roof, but I don't want to go to Mom's room yet. If she wakes up, she'll see that I'm upset, and she'll want to know why. What am I supposed to say then? *I'm upset because I'm afraid you're going to die.* I can't say that. There's never been anything I've held back from Mom, but I can't tell her this. I can't tell her I know about the chemotherapy, or that I'm scared she's dying and I don't know what's going to happen to her or me.

So I go to the roof.

Fischer joins me a few minutes later. "You came."

I nod. "Yeah." I'm not really sure what to say.

He sighs and leans against the roof's ledge. "Were you looking for something in particular in that file? If you have questions, it's always best to just ask them."

Except sometimes there are questions that are difficult to ask or illegal to discuss. I watch his face, trying to gauge what he's thinking, but his face is blank. Open. Encouraging. "I overheard the doctors that first day. They were arguing about giving Mom chemotherapy drugs. I didn't know there were chemo drugs around anymore. I was trying to find out whether the drugs had been approved."

He stays silent, and we look out across the city. It's quiet, with only a few people on the streets in this part of town.

One or two cars dot various places, but for the most part people don't drive anymore. Gas allowances are only given once a year, and each family is given a very small amount. People tend to use it for driving in the winter or heating their houses when it's cold.

A breeze tosses my hair into my face and I push it aside.

"You knew the drugs were requested?" he finally says.

I can't meet his eye, but I nod. "I saw her file the other day."

"There are a lot of things that most people don't know, Hana. I'm sorry you had to find out about the chemo drugs this way. You wouldn't have ever known about them if you hadn't heard the doctors that first day."

I nod. He makes a good point, but I do know about them now, and I won't ever forget. I want to know if they are approved, though. Why isn't he telling me that?

Still, I'm afraid to ask. What if he says they were denied?

"The request is still pending," he answers my unasked question.

Relief fills me up, but then I remember what he said a moment ago. "What other things don't people know?"

He watches me for a long time, but finally shakes his head. "This isn't the time or place for a conversation like that."

I stand up straighter and step toward him. "What do you mean? What's to hide?"

He sighs. "I shouldn't have said that."

"Well you did say it." I'm a little annoyed, but I know it's not fair to take it out on him. My real frustration comes from the issue with the chemo. This problem is too huge for me, and it hurts.

He watches me, his eyes soft. "You're right, I did say it. I'll tell you more if you want to know, but not here. Not in this place."

"What's wrong with this place?"

He glances around and then his gaze finds mine again. "Please trust me on this."

I turn my attention back to the city. Anger burns my insides. Anger at the doctors, at the mysteries, at the mutation. "How can I trust anyone?"

He scoots closer to the edge of the building and rests his elbows on the ledge, looking out over the city. "There *is* someone you can trust."

I snort. "Who?" It feels strange, being so cynical. I don't like this personality that's coming out.

He leans closer, his eyes wide and serious. "Have you ever heard of God, Hana?"

My breathing stills. God? I try to ignore the memories of my aunt dying when I was little. My parents had argued, because Mom wanted to know what happened to her sister after death. My dad yelled and said she was reincarnated, just like everyone else. I could tell Mom didn't agree, and there was some mention of God, but Dad was so mad Mom never brought it up again. I've never been sure of reincarnation since, but I haven't mentioned it. Religion is against the law, and Dad's a stickler for law-abidedness.

That's why we have meditation now. Besides the fact that religion separated the people of the country in the past, their belief in a God didn't do much for them. Meditation puts the responsibility on us, the people. We free our minds and spirits, and when our minds are clear we can find the answers we need.

"I guess so," I finally answer his question.

He nods and looks away. "There are answers to be found, if you want them."

Answers. That word intrigues me, because hadn't I just been thinking how there sure were a lot of unanswered questions floating around? Besides, if Mom might die, she would probably like to know what's going to happen to her afterward.

"Will you meet me?" he asks.

Meeting him would mean breaking the rules. Girls aren't allowed alone with boys. It isn't that the government is trying to prevent love; it's just that they're trying to prevent babies and extra mouths to feed. Back in the Early Days they had something called birth control pills. We don't have them anymore, but if we did, I'm sure the government would require we used them.

I swallow hard and look at the city one last time, and then I turn to him. I give one firm nod. "Yeah, I will."

11

Back in Mom's room her eyes flutter open, and she moans. It's a deep-throat moan of pain. My insides clench, and I rush to her side. "What's wrong, Mom?"

She swallows and glances around the room wildly. Finally, her eyes settle on me. "I'm fine, Hana. Sorry about that."

She doesn't seem fine. What if she'd awoken in pain, alone? Then I realize that she probably has, and I feel like I'm going to be sick. "Mom, are you OK? Do you need something? Maybe some water, or pain medicine?" At least there are still a few medicines that we can produce in our small country, which we know of, anyway.

"Water would be great. When the doctors come back I'll ask for more medicine."

I quickly fill a glass of water and hand it to her, but she only takes one small sip and sets it down.

"What time is it?" she asks.

I look at the clock on the wall. "It's a little before noon."

She frowns. "What day is it?"

"It's Sunday, Mom." She's obviously gotten her days mixed up, being in here for so long. "Hey, Mom, when will they let you go home? Can't they teach you how to eat this special diet at home?" If she isn't getting chemo drugs yet then I don't see why she needs to be here.

She shrugs a little, and I notice she winces with pain just doing that much. "I don't know. I haven't ever thought of it, but I'll ask. It does sound nice."

That lifts my spirits some. Having Mom home would be so great. I could still cook and clean, but I would be able to take care of her. We wouldn't have to come to the hospital every day, and we could all be together.

Fischer brings lunch around twelve. It's a fruit salad and a whole wheat roll. It doesn't seem very filling, but Mom says she doesn't have much of an appetite anyway.

"Would you like anything?" Fischer asks me. "We provide a meal for one visitor. Today is chili and cornbread."

I think about saying yes, but then I remember Mom can only eat fruits and vegetables. I don't want to make her hungry for something she can't have.

"No thanks," I say. "I have to meet my friend Jamie soon anyway. I can eat then."

Fischer smiles and ducks out. He doesn't show that we ever had a conversation before I came in. He doesn't show that he knows the government has the ability to help Mom get better but so far is choosing not to. He doesn't show that he knows my life is in turmoil.

I'm thankful for that.

"What are you and Jamie doing later?" Mom asks. She spears a strawberry and nibbles at it.

I don't want to go. I would rather stay here, with her. "It's the end of the week. We're going to the market to use up our food allowances."

My mom nods. "Get all that you can."

"Of course," I say, because of course I will. Why

would she feel the need to impart this to me? But then I realize I'm just being jumpy. She's being a mom. She doesn't have any authority anymore, and she's probably searching for any part of her life she can control.

And I thought *my* life was in turmoil. She must feel terrible, being cooped up in this room all day.

After she finishes her lunch, I kiss her on the cheek. "Maybe we'll find something good at the market I can bring you."

She smiles.

"Oh! I almost forgot." I pull a book from my bag. "Dad asked me to give this to you."

Her eyes light up like stars. "Oh, tell him thanks! This will give me something to do." My heart leaps at seeing her smile, but then she lets out a huge yawn. "Well, when I can stay awake anyway."

I'm reminded she isn't well.

I wave goodbye and start for home. Jamie will be watching for me, waiting to meet me at the sidewalk. We both look forward to our trips to market together. We get to browse new items, see new faces, and try new things. It's a nice break from our normally boring lives.

The food market is a ten minute walk from our block. This makes it even better, especially on days like today where the sun is shining and the weather is nice.

We walk in silence. I don't notice her tension at first, but then I see how her lips turn down at the corners, and her shoulders are rigid.

I suddenly want to talk, to say anything to break the uncomfortable nothingness between us.

Should I tell her about the strange lights I saw in the sky? But then I'd have to explain why I went to the levies in the first place. I think of telling her about Ava's brother, but that opens up a whole new set of questions I don't have answers for. When did I start keeping so many secrets from my best friend? A lump grows in my stomach. I don't like this feeling at all.

Then I think of something I can tell her. "I'm meeting this guy."

Jamie stops right in the middle of the sidewalk. Her eyebrows knit together and a deep frown mars her pretty face. "Huh?"

I glance around, suddenly self-conscience about the news. I propel her forward. "The medic I told you about from the hospital. I'm going to meet him."

Jamie doesn't say anything at first. I watch questions and judgments and emotions play through her blue eyes as she walks. Her eyes are cornflower blue—so light you want to go swimming in them. It's no wonder this Easton guy is hooked.

And that's why I know I can tell her about this. I keep her secret, she keeps mine.

"I thought you said it was nothing between you. You said you hadn't forgotten about Keegan."

"It's not like that. We're not meeting romantically. It's more like he's doing me a favor."

I remember his reference to God and I frown. I'm not sure how much of a favor it will be, but if he knows anything about chemo then I want to know, and if he knows anything about a real God, I want to know that, too.

Jamie cuts her eyes at me. "A favor? What is that supposed to mean?"

Maybe I shouldn't have brought it up, because now I'll have to go into those other subjects I didn't want to talk about. How much will I have to explain to help her understand? It's not that I don't trust her with the information, just that it all sounds crazy, and she already thought I was blowing the chemotherapy situation out of proportion.

I look around again. A few kids play in their yards, and a guard across the street waves at us. I smile and wave back. We're almost to the market.

"Do you remember what I told you about the chemo drugs?" I whisper.

She nods.

"The doctors requested them. I saw it on her chart. I was digging through her chart again, to see if they were approved yet. Fischer caught me looking, and he told me he could give me answers."

Her suspicious look doesn't fade like I'd hoped it would. "Fischer? That's his name?"

"Yeah."

Jamie sighs. "Are you sure he's not just trying to get you alone?"

"No!" I say it too loudly and glance around again. I'm paranoid, as if the guard from the other night has been following me around, hoping to catch me break another rule. She did say they'd be watching.

"He's not," I say more quietly. "I just want to know more about the drugs. Maybe he knows how we can get some."

Jamie doesn't stop frowning, but we're at the market now so our conversation stops.

12

Tables of succulent fruits and vegetables line one side of the square-shaped outdoor market. It's set up in what used to be an old parking lot, with different sections for different food types. "I'm starving," I say, fingering a ripe peach. "I skipped lunch."

"Get one," Jamie says, glancing around. She seems distracted.

"My dad would probably have a heart attack if I even thought about eating a fruit he didn't grow." We both laugh, probably because we can both picture it.

I head to the grains instead. Sugars, flours, salts, and other spices and baking contents fill two tables. I stock up on flour and yeast, even though I can't help looking at the brown sugar. We rarely get sweets because sugar is so expensive. It's regulated by the government.

I see Jamie at another table further down. She smiles and laughs, and then I realize she's talking to Easton. He runs a produce table along with his dad. No wonder Jamie likes coming to market so much. How did I not realize this before?

Curiosity hits me again, and I weave in and out of the small crowd.

Easton's dad says something to Jamie, but I'm too far back to hear him.

Jamie throws back her head and laughs. It appears she's more familiar with him and his family than I knew. Maybe I should just leave them alone.

I step back into the crowd, deciding to keep an eye on her from a distance.

It looks like she's bought a basket of eggs. Too bad I didn't think of that before I spent my allowances on grain. Sometimes I try to talk Dad into letting us get a chicken with our food allowance, but so far he's said no. I don't know what the big deal is, since it would save us in the long run. We'd always have eggs available, and we wouldn't have to spend allowance on them. Not that we ever go hungry. Resources may be tight, but the Greaters make sure all the Middles get an even share. Even the Lessers get an even share among themselves, though I think they could probably have a little more. It might motivate them to make more of themselves.

At the last minute, I remember I wanted to look for something for Mom. My allowance is gone, and guilt settles in my stomach. It's silly because really, what can I buy Mom, food-wise? She's on a strict diet, and the hospital provides her meals. I'll use my entertainment allowance to buy her more books instead. She'll appreciate that more.

I finish browsing the other tables and look around to find Jamie. Not surprisingly, she's still talking to Easton.

"Hey, are you ready to go?" I ask.

"Sure," she says. "Mr. Denzine, this is my best friend, Hana."

Easton's dad and I smile at each other.

"Hey, Hana," Easton says.

I smile at him, too, but we don't speak beyond that.

"I guess I'll see you later," Jamie says.

Easton nods. "Right. See you later." His eyes dance and his lips are shaped in a full-fledged smile.

I frown. There's something about this that I don't like. We start back toward home, and I can't keep my questions to myself. "Are you meeting him later?"

Jamie's head whips to look at me. "What?"

"He seemed to be getting at something when he said he'd see you later. It just bothered me."

"Hana, don't worry about us. We'll be OK." She barges ahead, and I have to race to keep up with her longer steps.

"Sorry," I say. "I don't mean to butt in. I just don't want anything bad to happen. What if you get caught?"

She doesn't look at me when she says, "We won't get caught, Hana. You don't have time for me, and I understand that, but you don't understand some things. I wouldn't have to sneak around with him if you were ever around to hang out with us. I've always done that for you and Keegan, you know."

I stop like I've been hit in the gut. Is that how she's always looked at it? I was using her so I could hang out with Keegan?

She goes a few steps before she realizes I've stopped. She looks to the sky and lets out a long, pent up breath. "I'm sorry," she finally says. "That was selfish and stupid, and I know it."

I watch her back, which is still turned to me. "Is that all you were doing? Being a buffer for me and Keegan? I always thought we were hanging out because we were friends."

She turns now. Tears gather in her eyes. "Of course not. We were all friends, I know. It's just that I wish you could share that with me and Easton, too. I know you need to be with your mom." She shrugs. "I just wish it was different."

I want to shout, *you* wish it was different? How do you think *I* feel? But I'm not really mad at her. I love my best friend. Instead of shouting, I step toward her and hug her around my bag of grains and her baskets of eggs. An egg tips out and cracks on the pavement.

We laugh nervously.

"I'm sorry," she says.

"That's OK, Jamie. I'm sorry about being nosey."

"You weren't being nosey. You were looking after me," she says. She tips her head to the side and smiles timidly. "But would you like to hang out with us? Maybe just once?"

Hang out with Jamie and Easton? Easton is interested in agriculture. He's tall and gangly, and he snorts when he laughs. He reminds me of Dad.

But Jamie's eyes are so hopeful, and I love her and can't imagine letting her down. There's no way I can say no. "Sure. Just tell me when."

13

Ava catches up to me after school a few days later. "Can I talk to you?" Her face is all screwed up with worry.

I've been waiting outside for Jamie, but she hasn't showed up. We haven't exactly been meditating like we used to, and so our routine has puttered out.

"Of course," I say, walking with Ava now. "What's wrong?"

"I've been thinking about the night Markus got hurt."

"Yeah?"

A group of kids walks near us. She glances at them, and then whispers, "Why would he be in a tree?"

I frown. "What do you mean?"

"He was out after curfew. Why would he go outside to climb a tree?"

"Maybe he wanted to be alone. You share a room, right?"

She shakes her head. "No, that can't be it. He's never tried to avoid me before. Besides, I wasn't even in my room. I was with Mom and Dad downstairs. He knew that. We all thought he had gone upstairs. He deliberately misled us."

Her words make sense. What had he gone outside to do?

"Do you have any theories?" I ask.

"I don't know what he was breaking curfew for, but it had to be something important don't you think? He broke the law, yes, but they wouldn't keep us from seeing him just because he was out late. He was either doing something really bad, or he saw something really bad. They don't want him to tell us what happened that night."

Ava makes a good point. Worry starts worming its way through my head.

The line between her eyebrows disappears, even though the wrinkles at her eyes don't. "You agree with me."

"Yes, I agree with you." There's something strange about the whole situation.

The relief is evident on her face. She thought I would say she was crazy—like Jamie thought about me when I told her about the chemo.

"I think I should tell someone."

"No!" I shout it too quickly and too loudly, and the kids in front of us stop talking and look at us.

I grab Ava's arm and drag her away. "You can't do that, Ava. If something really *is* going on, and you suspect it, they're going to lock you away just like Markus."

Her eyes widen and her face goes pale. "They couldn't do that, could they?"

I'm beginning to question exactly what the Greaters *can* do. "Yes, they can, and they will, Ava. You have to stay away from them."

Her eyes stay glued to mine for what feels like eternity. She bites her lower lip and finally shrugs. "OK, I guess, but what am I supposed to do with this idea?"

Now it's my turn to glance around. When I'm sure

no one is watching us I say, "Figure out where he was, what he was doing—what he saw. Find his trail. You can figure it out."

She frowns. "I don't know if I can."

"You can and you have to. If you want to figure out what's going on, I'll help you."

"How?"

Good question. "I'm not sure, but we'll figure it out."

A guard is walking down the street. She's not watching us, but I don't want to take any chances. "I'll talk to you tomorrow, Ava," I say, and I leave her with a wave and hurry home.

Dad sits at the table grading papers. "Would it be OK if I didn't go to the hospital today?" I only have two days before my entertainment allowance expires, and I want to get Mom those books before then. Besides, I've promised to hang out with Jamie and Easton later this afternoon.

Dad glances up from his paper in surprise. "You don't want to go?"

"I have some stuff I promised Mom I would do."

His face relaxes some, like he's glad I'm not tired of going to the hospital.

I'm surprised myself when I realize I'm *not* tired of going to the hospital.

"That's fine, Hana. I'll go." He puts his paper down and stands up, slipping his feet into his shoes. "So what are your plans?"

"I'm going to The Shops to get Mom some books. Jamie will probably come with me."

My dad nods, and I slip out the door once I put my things down. I hope Jamie doesn't mind coming with me before we meet up with Easton.

Since talking with Ava I feel jittery. Out of sorts. Paranoid. The more I learn about what's wrong with our country, the more I wonder about everything I've been taught. Is everyone in on a conspiracy? Is no one good?

I shake off the bad feelings and knock on Jamie's door. Her mom answers and smiles at me. She doesn't speak, just points me upstairs. The stairs creak as I climb.

"Jamie?" I call out.

Her head pops out of the closet. "Hey, Hana," she says quietly. Has she been crying? "You're early."

"Do you want to go to The Shops with me before we meet Easton? I want to get my mom some books."

She wrings her hands together, her gaze darting around the room. Finally, she nods. "Sure. That'd be great."

I wonder if she and her mom had a fight or something.

"Let me grab my stuff." Her hands shake as she stuffs things in a small purse.

I frown. "Are you OK?"

"Yep, fine. Let's get out of here, OK?"

"Yeah, sure." I follow her downstairs and wave at her mom as we pass. Once we're outside in the open, she seems to relax a little. Maybe she and her mom really did have a fight, and now she's glad to be away. Still, I want to make sure. "Are you sure you're OK?"

She glances up and down the street about a half dozen times. "Yes. Or I will be. So, how did your pow-wow with the medic go?"

I shake my head. "I haven't seen him yet. He hasn't brought it up again, and I haven't asked."

"Oh?" she says. "It's better that way." She doesn't

expound, and I stare at her, worried. Something is definitely bothering her, and I'm determined to get her to tell me before we get home.

The Shops is a group of old buildings that used to be called a mini mall. We try to use the old buildings around town that are still in good shape, even though most of them are more than two hundred years old. There's a clothing shop, an apothecary, a bookstore, a toy shop, a restaurant, and a bakery. We head to the bookstore first.

"I'm surprised you have any entertainment allowance left," Jamie says.

I frown at her. "I've been at the hospital for more than a week straight." It's not like her to forget something like that.

Her expression clouds and then clears. "Right. Sorry. I heard at school that Mr. Dillard is making new soaps out of flower extract or something. The girls say it makes your skin smell good."

"Like perfume?"

She nods.

Perfume is rare and expensive. My mom has a bottle she keeps on her dresser, but she hardly ever wears it. If I don't spend all my allowance on books, I might head to the apothecary to smell it.

The aroma of musty old books drifts in the air as we push through the door of the bookstore. I browse the selection, and Jamie breaks out of her odd behavior long enough to recommend a few titles for Mom. They're really good choices, and I add them to my small stack.

A big man in dirty clothes barges through the door. He carries a large box of books. "New stuff just in," he says to Mrs. Baily, the bookkeeper's wife. He sets his load on the counter and then mops his forehead with a towel.

Mrs. Baily's small eyes light up. "Where'd these ones come from?"

"A dig about a hundred miles north of here. I haven't gone through them yet, though, so you'll have to weed out what stays and what goes."

Mrs. Baily nods. "No problem."

We don't have the supplies to print books anymore, so we rely on old books from the Early Days that people dig up. Some books aren't allowed to stay, though. Books that deal with touchy subjects like politics, religion, and rebellion are burned.

I've never actually seen books right off a dig, and I'm intrigued. "Can I look at them?" I ask Mrs. Baily.

She smiles like she understands my fascination and nods. "You can look, but don't touch. They haven't been cleaned or sorted yet."

Some of the books have dull, single-colored hard covers, but others have bright, flashy covers, and I wonder how they printed pictures like that right on a book.

Mrs. Baily sorts through them while I browse.

One book is different than the others. It looks soft, like leather. I reach my hand out to touch it. It's covered in dust, and I can't read the title so I brush my hand over it.

Holy Bible.

Mrs. Baily gasps and snatches it away. She holds it to her chest, her eyes wide with terror.

I pull back, surprised at her odd behavior.

"This one's got to be burned," she says. "You shouldn't look at it, and don't mention it!"

I frown, my face contorting in confusion. "I

understand," I finally mutter. But I can't make sense of her reaction. I don't even know those words. Holy Bible. Why would they make her so afraid?

Her behavior gives me the creeps, and I want to get out of there. We pay for the books and head outside.

"Did you see that?" I ask.

"Hmm?" Jamie says.

Obviously, she hadn't. I shake my head, glad to put it behind me. "Do you want to smell Mr. Dillard's new soap?"

She frowns like she doesn't know what I'm talking about, but then her face clears. "Oh, right. Sure. Let's go."

A small bell tied to the door of Mr. Dillard's shop jingles when the door opens. The tinkling sound makes me happy, lessening the bad feeling I got from the bookstore.

"Good afternoon, girls," Mr. Dillard says. "How are you today?"

The apothecary sells herbs, candles, soaps, and cleaners. Everything he makes comes from things grown in the ground. He looks like he's about a hundred, with wrinkles on his forehead, cheeks, neck, arms, and even his hands, but Mom says he's only in his sixties.

"We heard you had some new flower soaps."

He grins, and I notice he doesn't have any teeth. "It's called perfumed soap. It used to be common in the Early Days, but it's not so common these days."

He pulls something off the shelf and gives it to us to smell. The scent of fresh lilacs meets my nose.

"What do you think?" he asks.

"I like it," I say. I hand him the rest of my

allowance. "How much is it? Does this cover it?"

He smiles and nods. "This will be fine."

Jamie smiles tightly and thrusts the soap back at me. Her face looks a little green.

We hurry outside and I grab her arm. "Are you sick or something? What's wrong, Jamie? You haven't been acting right all day, and I need to know you're OK."

She glances around and starts walking again.

"Jamie!" I say, hurrying to catch up.

"I really think you shouldn't meet that guy alone."

This again? "What are you talking about?"

"Don't meet any guy alone, not even Keegan."

"Jamie, you're not making any sense!"

She stops now and looks around one last time. She leans close to me and I see the tears in her eyes. "Being alone with a guy is bad, Hana. I don't know what to do."

My stomach drops to my knees and I hold my breath as she says her next words.

"I think I'm pregnant."

14

Pregnant? I can't imagine my best friend being pregnant. We're still in school! We haven't taken our Tests yet, let alone finished our college training.

Then another thought hits me. They're going to make her abort the baby. You aren't allowed to have children before the given time. If she refuses, they will lower her status, and she won't be allowed to take the Test.

The thought of Jamie in a Lesser city horrifies me, but the alternative is much worse.

"What will you do?" I ask. I'm afraid to hear her answer. I'm afraid she'll say she's keeping the baby, and I'll never see her again. Middles aren't allowed to enter the Lesser cities. But I'm more afraid she'll say she's *not* keeping the baby. I don't care what the government says, the thought of killing a little baby makes my stomach hurt. It can't be right, no matter what they say it does for society.

She studies me for a minute and then looks straight ahead. "I won't abort the baby. I won't do it."

I sigh with relief. Somehow, never seeing her again is more palatable to me then thinking my best friend is a baby killer.

She glances at me when she hears the sigh. "Do you think it's the right thing?" Her eyes are unsure, scared.

"Yes!" I say, way too quickly. I take a moment to

figure things out. "Yes, it's the right thing. I don't know why or how, but I know it's got to be the right thing."

Jamie nods. "Me, too. I haven't told anyone yet. I wasn't really sure at first, but I'm pretty sure now."

I think of Easton. I don't know him well at all. How could this have happened? "What will Easton say about keeping the baby?"

"He'll go with me. I'm sure of it. He loves me."

Her words stick out to me. *He'll go with me.* Because they'll be forced to leave the city. But will he go with her? I sure hope so. A strange fear creeps into my belly, and I close my eyes against the dizziness that hits me.

"You won't tell anyone, will you?"

The fact she doesn't know for sure I'll keep her secret hurts me, but then I consider the position she's in. If I think *I'm* scared and confused, how does she feel? As soon as anyone finds out she'll be sent away. The longer we can keep it quiet, the longer she'll get to stay in Middle City 3.

"No, I won't tell. How long do you think you can keep it a secret, though?"

I have no idea about things like babies and pregnancy. I've never actually known anyone who was having a baby.

Jamie shrugs. "I don't know." She covers her face with her hands. "I don't know how this happened. I'm so stupid."

I want to tell her, *yeah, pretty stupid,* but I don't. I doubt it would help the situation.

"They'll try and make you do it, you know? They won't let you go so easily." She's from a good family, and she makes good grades in school. They won't let her go without a fight. If she aborts the baby, she can stay, even though she would be on probation. They will try to make her abort.

She grinds her teeth together. "I won't give in. I'll prepare myself for the worst future possible—living in filth, or poverty, or...or alone." The last word comes out as a whisper.

We're almost home now. I stop and give Jamie a hug. "I'm glad you told me, Jamie. I'm glad you're making the decision you are. You'll do the right thing—we're too much alike, and I know what I'd do."

Jamie smiles, but her eyes pin me down. "That's what I'm afraid of, Hana. Don't meet that guy alone. Please!'

I freeze, appalled at the thought of going *there* with Fischer.

"We don't even know each other!" I say. "And I told you it's not like that." I can tell my ears are red because they burn like fire.

Jamie studies me another short moment and shrugs again. "I'm just saying." She hugs me one last time. We're in front of her house now. "Thanks for taking me with you. It's good to know I'm not alone."

"You're not," I say.

We both stop talking when her mom steps outside. "Jamie, that boy is in the backyard. Did you invite him over again?" It's obvious her mom isn't very happy with the relationship. How's she going to take it when she finds out what's been happening between them?

"We're going to hang out," Jamie says. "Hana will be with us."

Her mom glances between the two of us. Finally, she sighs. "He can't stay long, do you understand?"

Jamie nods. "OK, Mom."

She goes back inside the house.

My head spins. "Have you told him yet?"

Jamie shakes her head. "No. I was going to tell him today."

Panic chokes me. "What?"

"Please, Hana? I can't do it alone."

I shake my head, trying to get the cobwebs dislodged. "Fine. Tell me what you want me to do, and I'll do it."

15

Questions play through my mind. What if Easton doesn't support her? What if he does? Will they get married? Live in some Lesser apartment in the housing developments? Will Jamie have to get one of the Lesser-approved jobs, like cleaning the streets? Will they have to lock all their doors at night to keep other Lessers from breaking in and stealing from them or killing them in their sleep?

I've always wanted to help the Lessers, to promote their ability to do good. But now? Faced with the possibility of my best friend being one of them, I'm terrified by the thought of them. Everything I've been taught comes rushing back to me. Drugs, alcohol, crime. How will Jamie survive in such a terrible life? Will my career in Middle government include helping my best friend? I feel weak and old, like I can't bear to carry even the skin that's on my bones. I can't take any more surprises in my life.

We round the house and Easton sits in the grass against a tree. Jamie's backyard looks exactly like mine, and every other yard on our street—a small square of grass enclosed by a rickety, old fence.

Easton smiles when he sees us and shoots to his feet. "Hi," he says to Jamie alone.

Smitten is the word that comes to mind.

She smiles back, tucking her long brown hair behind her ear. "Hi."

We stand in an awkward huddle for a second, but Jamie breaks the ice by sitting beside the tree. "How's your afternoon been?" she asks.

As if she didn't just see him at school two hours ago.

Easton shrugs easily. "Fine. I helped my dad at the market until I came here. What about you?"

Jamie glances at me and then looks back to Easton. "It's been good. We went shopping."

He grins wider. "Yeah, girls like shopping."

He's such a dork. I don't see what Jamie sees in him at all. The whole backyard seems to be emitting discomfort. Ten feet away is the comfort of my own backyard. How terrible would it be if I just got up and sat in my own grass?

"Did you buy anything?" he asks.

"No, but Hana got some books and soap."

He nods.

I wonder if this is what all of their time together has been like, but then I think of Jamie's news, and my cheeks burn. Why doesn't she just get it over with?

"Your dad's the dean of the agricultural school, right?" His bug eyes turn on me.

"Yep."

"My dad says that when they were in school together your dad could make anything grow. He said they called it a green thumb. My dad says I might be the next dean!"

My dad? I've never thought of him being someone's hero before. It's a funny thought. "I guess he is pretty good at growing things."

"After we Test, I guess I'll get to know him better, huh?"

His carefree words are almost too heavy to handle,

but since Jamie hasn't told him the truth yet, I'm not sure how to respond. "Right, because you want to do agriculture."

Jamie shifts in the grass, groaning a little. "Do we have to talk about the Test? Who really cares about it anyway?"

Easton's eyebrows shoot up. He is obviously confused — everyone cares about the Test.

If the situation wasn't so serious, I might think it was kind of funny. Smitten boy confused by pretty girl.

"Sure, we don't have to talk about it," he says. "We can talk about whatever you want."

Jamie huffs again. She keeps her eyes downcast, picking at the skin around her fingers. "I actually have something to tell you, Easton. It's important."

I watch his eyebrows come together now. His confusion has deepened.

Jamie swallows hard and glances between me and Easton. "I think I'm pregnant."

The words come out so softly that I almost don't hear them myself. I can tell Easton didn't hear because he's not flipping out yet, and Easton definitely strikes me as the flipping out type.

"Did you hear me?" Jamie asks. Irritation makes her voice rise.

Before Easton can answer, she says more loudly, "I said I think I'm pregnant."

His face goes whiter than the snow in February. "Huh?"

Jamie starts to cry, an angry frown on her face. "That's all you have to say?"

He shakes his head quickly. "No, I mean, are you sure?"

"Pretty sure."

He glances at me, his eyes wide and petrified. "Did you know about this?"

"She told me this afternoon," I say. My stomach drops, and I don't see the humor in the situation anymore. She's told him. It's real now. My best friend is pregnant, and our lives are about to be changed forever, one way or the other.

"What are you going to do?" Easton says.

Jamie sniffles a few more times. "I'm going to keep the baby. I hoped you'd agree with me on that."

"I'll do whatever you want me to!"

His passion surprises me. Maybe Jamie is right about him.

"You know what that means though, right?" I ask. I feel obligated to give him a reality check. "You won't get to Test for agriculture. You'll be sent away to a Lesser city." I can't picture Easton as a Lesser. Everything about him reminds me of Dad, and that picture doesn't fit at all.

I watch the realization set in. His eyes lose some of their light. His shoulders sag a fraction lower. It's like I've just cut away a few years of his life.

"I don't care," he says. He takes Jamie's hands. "I'll stay with you no matter what."

She smiles through her tears. "I knew you would."

"I love you, Jamie."

"I love you, too." They stare at each other, Jamie crying, Easton ashen.

Now my backyard looks doubly tempting.

Jamie's mom storms through the backyard. "Jamie!" she shrieks.

Jamie and Easton's hands fly apart like two negative magnets. Red floods Jamie's face and Easton stands quickly. "I guess I should go," he says.

Jamie's mom glares at him as he makes his hasty retreat, and then she stomps to the tree. "What was all that about?"

Jamie wipes her tears and stands up. "Nothing Mom. It was nothing."

Her mom isn't at all convinced.

I stand, too. "I better get home, Jamie. I'll see you later."

No one looks at me, so I sprint across the yard and into the safety of my own house. I peek out the window and see mother and daughter fighting. Her mom is obviously suspicious of the whole Jamie/Easton relationship. Jamie pushes past her mom and storms into her backdoor.

I can't help but wonder how long Jamie will be able to keep her secret.

16

I'm glad for the quiet of the hospital lobby today. No one met me after school, and I came immediately after class. I'm thankful to be able to visit with Mom alone and give her the books I bought her. I want to laugh with her and see her smile. I don't want to think about Jamie, a baby, Easton, or Lessers.

Fischer meets me in the hallway with a smile, as usual. "Hey, Hana. How are you today?"

Terrible. "Good, how are you?"

"Doing great. Are you still up for that class?"

Of course I know what he's talking about, but why is he talking in code? I glance around and see Dr. Bentford bent over a desk in an alcove behind Fischer's work area. "Absolutely. When is it again?"

"I can't remember. I'll let you know before you leave. Don't leave without seeing me."

"Right. I won't."

He moves on to his work station, and I consider the meeting with him. I feel better equipped to deal with the problems surrounding a corrupt government today. It's less painful than finding out my best friend isn't exactly who I thought she was. I hurry to Mom's room.

"Hana!" she says. She's sitting up today, nibbling on fruit. Maybe this means progress.

Guilt hits me for not visiting yesterday. "I brought you these." I pull the books I bought from my bag.

Her smile lights up the room. "Hana, these are great. Thank you so much." Her voice sounds happy enough, but she looks pale. Her eyes are pinched.

"Do you need anything, Mom? Water or medicine?"

"No, no. I'm OK."

But I can tell she's not.

"What do they say about the nutrition treatments? Did you ever ask about coming home?"

"I did ask, but they said it's best to monitor me here."

She didn't answer my first question. I can tell the nutrition treatments aren't working, and fear bubbles up in my stomach. It feels like stew when it's left too long on the stove—thick and inedible.

I force the thoughts away and sit in the chair beside the bed. "Have you read any of these before?"

"No, I've never seen them."

That's not surprising, since there are only a few copies of any given book that's been found in a dig.

"Jamie helped me pick them out. She knows you almost as well as I do."

My mom smiles at that. "I'm a little surprised she hasn't come with you to visit."

"She's been busy lately," I say. *Busy doing things she shouldn't be doing and getting herself into a mess.*

Maybe I shouldn't have kept her from coming with me all those times she offered. The thought takes my breath away. *Is her pregnancy partly my fault?*

I shake myself. I don't want to think about this here.

"Your friend Ava's been visiting me, too, while she's here to see her brother. There's something strange going on there."

I'm intrigued that she says this. "Do you think so?"

"I don't know what it is, but why wouldn't they let the family see him? It doesn't make any sense." She takes a shaky breath and closes her eyes.

As much as I want to get her opinion on this, I'm more worried about her actions. "Are you OK, Mom?"

She nods but keeps her eyes closed.

"It hurts, doesn't it?"

My mom doesn't say anything and I know this means yes.

Seeing her like this hurts me. I can't stand the thought of her in pain. My eyes burn and my stomach clenches.

The door slides open and Dr. Lane walks in. "Hi Hana. How are you?"

"Mom's in pain," I say, ignoring her question. "Isn't there something we can give her?"

Dr. Lane frowns. She checks Mom's temperature and does a routine examination. "Would you like more pain medicine?"

Mom nods silently, and Dr. Lane marks something on Mom's chart. "I'll let Fischer know, and he'll be in shortly."

Mom's eyes are closed again.

I glance at Dr. Lane's retreating back. I want to know more. "I'll be right back, Mom."

I catch Dr. Lane in the hallway. "How's she doing? With the mutation, I mean?"

Dr. Lane glances at the door to Mom's room. "Have you asked her those questions?"

"Yes, she won't say anything. The treatments aren't working, are they?"

Dr. Lane sighs. "Not as well as I'd like. I haven't

lost hope, though. I'm trying to get some other things worked out."

Chemo drugs. An ember of hope flames to life. "OK, thanks."

Dr. Lane smiles. "Fischer will be back in a bit with the pain meds."

I slip back into Mom's room and wait for Fischer. My mom's already asleep, and my head swims with the knowledge that she's questioning the actions of the Greaters where Markus Huckleberry is concerned. My parents have always supported the government every step of the way. I got that from them, I guess. If Mom is questioning them now, though, what does that mean for me?

Fischer comes in a few minutes later. He injects a yellow liquid into Mom's IV line, and then pulls a paper from his pocket and hands it to me.

"I hope you'll be there," he says quietly. "There will be people who can answer your questions better than I can."

I'm surprised because I thought it would be just me and him. Embarrassment hits me, but I hide it by looking down. At least he doesn't know I thought it'd be just the two of us. But then I think of Jamie's warning and a silent relief floods through me.

Still, I'm nervous at the same time. There are others? People who know strange things are going on, and who know the government isn't all it promises to be?

This thought strikes me as eerie, like I've just learned about an alternate world right in my own backyard.

I nod. "I'll be there."

"Good. I'll see you around." He checks Mom one

last time and then backs from the room.

He's so quiet when he moves. So gentle. Caring.

I'm glad he's taking care of Mom. It reminds me of Ava—a natural caretaker. I admire him.

I unfold the note. *871 Kensington Ave. 11 PM. Tonight.*

I swallow hard. Let's see if I get caught after curfew this time.

17

I slip into the dark backyard as quietly as I can. I'm not exactly a pro at sneaking around, and I hope no one can hear my thundering heartbeat. A bright moon lights my pathway, and I can see clearly. That's good and bad. Good because I can see, but bad because so can others. The address Fischer gave to me is familiar. Kensington Avenue is across town. Its houses are older, falling apart. No one lives there, or at least I thought no one did.

I've thought the whole day about the best way to get there. Most of my path will be lined with alleys. That makes for great cover.

A stray cat meows at me, and I nearly shout out. What's a stray doing around here anyway? We don't have many animals in our city. The Greaters say we barely have enough food to feed ourselves. We can't be feeding pets, too. In fact, most pets end up as meals during the winter months.

I'm three blocks from home when I see the first guard. It's a man, I think, and he's wearing strange glasses on his eyes. I've never seen glasses like that—kind of like I'd never seen the little machine the woman guard had the last time I was out past curfew. He casually scans the streets, like he doesn't really expect to find anything.

He turns my way and I press myself behind a tree, hoping the trunk hides me. He scans the street and then moves on. I take a deep breath and keep moving. How long will it take me to get there? I'm not entirely sure. I've never been to Kensington Avenue, especially not in the middle of the night.

I dart between hiding spots, camouflaging myself from a guard here and there. It's not nearly as hard as I thought it would be. I shouldn't be surprised, since it was so easy getting out of the house. My dad never suspected a thing when we said goodnight. I guess it's the same for getting across town. The guards don't actually expect to see anyone out in the dark.

I get there within twenty minutes. I'm actually a few minutes late, I think, but that can't really matter. I was right about the houses. They're old and falling apart. The shutters hang at odd angles, and most of the windows don't have glass. I wonder why Fischer and his people would want to meet me here, but then I realize. The place is abandoned.

I scurry down the side walk, glancing at dilapidated number signs hanging on the fronts of the houses. Where is 871? It has to be around here somewhere.

I look away from a sign numbered 7-9-0 and right into the face of a guard. My scream pierces the night, but it doesn't affect the guard.

"What are you doing here?" he demands.

My mind sputters and moans and dies, and no words come from my mouth. I don't know what to do, but I can't let this guard know why I'm really here.

I do the only thing I can think to do. I run as fast as I can.

The guard's footsteps pound against the broken sidewalk behind me. I hear him speaking, and I wonder to whom. Is there another guard with him? I didn't see anyone else.

"We have a runner on Kensington Avenue. She's headed toward the river."

The words seem odd, detached. *I'm* the runner. *I'm* headed toward the river. He's talking about me.

I jog down an alley and will myself to go faster. Wind stings my eyes, and I wipe a stray tear from my cheek. If he thinks I'm heading to the river, and that's where he's sending backup, then I'm definitely not going there. I come out of the alley and take a left, going back in my original direction, just on a different street.

"Stop!" the guard yells. "By order of the Guards!"

I don't stop. I have to get away. What will they do if they catch me? Will they put me in jail? Make me a Lesser? Will they search every house on Kensington Avenue and find Fischer and his people? What if we're all caught?

I wonder briefly where the instinct to run came from. I've never run from someone before—I'm more of a stay and work things out kind of girl.

My lungs burn and my throat hurts from breathing so hard. I know I have to get away, but I have a feeling he's gaining on me. At the last minute, I dart into an old house. This may be the dumbest thing I've ever done, but I noticed half the houses don't have windows. If I can make it to one and climb out another way, it might buy me a better lead.

I hurry through the sprawling house, looking for a front window. Glass and trash and debris litter the wooden floor, and I see the front door a few feet ahead. The window I need is right beside it, so I lunge.

It's then I realize I don't hear footsteps behind me. Did the guard follow me into the house?

Hands like iron bracelets clamp around my wrists. "Just what do you think you're doing out here, girl?" the guard says. He huffs and puffs with exertion, but he doesn't really sound upset.

I have to come up with a story fast. I can't exactly say I'm on my way to meet with a group who will tell me all about religion and the corruption of our government.

"I was meeting my boyfriend," I say. I'm huffing and puffing, too, and my legs feel like deflated balloons. I fall to my knees.

"Some guy he is, letting you get chased through the streets and not helping you out. I think you'd better drop that one."

At least he believes my story, but guilt nags at my brain for the lie.

"What are you going to do to me?" I ask between gulps of air.

He leans against the house, still breathing hard. "I've already called for backup, so I can't let you go. You'll have to make a statement. You'll probably get your entertainment allowances revoked for the month, and you'll get a mark on your record. Three marks and you get demoted." He squats in front of me. "Trust me, girl. There isn't a boy in the world worth that."

Why isn't he surprised? I was shocked when I found out Jamie was meeting Easton, but maybe it happens all the time. Maybe *I'm* the strange one.

"Have you got your ID on you?" he asks.

"In my pocket."

He reaches in my pocket and pulls out the small plastic card. He punches numbers into the same kind of machine the other guard had. I want to ask him what it is, but I'm not sure the guards look kindly on inquisitive law breakers. Then again, he was much more conversational then the other guard had been.

"What is that thing?" I ask.

"It's called a pocket scanner. It's like a mini computer. It lets me check your file for other violations." He stares at the screen for a moment and then frowns. "You were issued a warning a week ago for being out after curfew. Didn't learn your lesson?"

"That was different. My mom's in the hospital. She has the mutation, and I stayed late to be with her. It was stupid, I know."

He watches me silently. Finally, he sighs. "Yeah, it was stupid, but I know how you feel. My sister died of the mutation when we were kids."

Tears swell in my eyes. That is exactly what I don't want to hear, someone else dying from the mutation.

Still, at least he believes me—again. Are all the guards as gullible as this one?

A moment later I hear a rumbling noise down the street, and a car pulls in front of the house.

The guard helps me stand up. "Here's your ride, kid. Stay out of trouble, and drop the boyfriend. He's no good."

"Thanks," I say.

I stare at the car, chewing on my lip. The last time I rode in a car was once when Mom's sister visited from Middle City 1.

The guard helps me into the back seat, and my stomach is in knots. What are they going to do with me? Where are they going to take me? What will my parents think of me? They'll think I was meeting a boy, and they'll want to know who. People will say I'm acting out because of Mom's sickness.

I half-snort as I realize that last part is kind of true.

I *am* doing this because of Mom's illness, only it's not in rebellion to the mutation itself, just the Greaters' treatment of it. Of course I can't be sure, but I think I'm going to get off pretty easy. And since I didn't get the information I needed, I think it's safe to say I'm going to do it again the first chance I get.

18

I've never even seen the guard station before tonight. It's really a quaint, quiet-looking, brick building. Nothing extraordinary. Not even menacing. There are no barbed-wire fences or barred windows. In fact, a beautiful flower bed blooms around the left side of the building.

It strikes me as odd how some things survived the Early Days, and other things didn't. Things like flower beds and colleges made it through, but things like pets and freedom didn't.

My own observation surprises me. Freedom? When did I start feeling like I wasn't free? Maybe when Ava was denied the freedom to see her brother, or our entire nation was denied the freedom to look for a possible God.

"State your name, miss," a man behind a desk says. It snaps me back to reality.

"Hana Norfolk."

"Why were you out this evening, Hana?" Again, this guard isn't mean or threatening. If I had to guess, I'd say he was bored and tired.

"I was meeting a boy from school."

"Boy's name?"

I freeze. I can't give Fischer's name of course. First of all, he's not in my school, and second of all, it will put him under surveillance, which he doesn't need.

"Don't worry, Hana," the guard says. "Most girls

don't give up their boys. Just give me a name."

This man thinks nothing of me lying on the record? That seems wrong somehow, but I'm grateful. "Jasper Hazel." I could kick myself as soon as the words are out. Jasper is a boy from my school. What if they question him? What if he gets in trouble? Why didn't I just make up a name?

The guard doesn't notice my distress and just scribbles my answers on his notepad. "A guard will escort you home. He'll have to speak to your parents though."

I swallow hard. What will Dad say? He'll definitely be mad, especially after I was stopped a few nights ago. He's going to be speechless. I've never really caused a moment's trouble, always playing by the rules, doing things the safe way. And now I've gotten into trouble twice in one week.

When we finish with the report, a guard takes me to another car. She lets me out of my cuffs and points in my face. "You're lucky they're letting you go," she says. "You ran away. You could have been locked up for days."

My stomach drops. *Locked up?*

We make the rest of the ride in the quiet of night. I've never been through the city at night, and it's eerie, seeing house after dark house. I think about Fischer. Does he know why I didn't make it, or does he assume I changed my mind? Worse, did he get caught himself?

At my house the guard knocks on the door loud enough to wake Dad, but hopefully not the neighbors. The door flies open, and Dad stands in the doorway disheveled and confused.

His eyes land on me and his shock is apparent for all to see. "What's going on here?"

"Your daughter was out after curfew, Mr. Norfolk. I'm afraid she was going to meet a boy."

His eyes widen wildly, a thick wrinkle forming between his brows.

I can almost hear his thoughts, *What about Keegan?* It's no secret to either of our families that we intend to be together.

"This is her first offense, so we're letting her off easy. She ran from the guards, though, so next time it will be a lot worse." I flinch, wishing she would've left off that last sentence.

My dad's nostrils flare and he pulls me inside. "There won't be a next time. I'm sorry for your trouble."

The guard nods and retreats to her car.

My dad closes the door and stares at his feet for a long time. When he raises his head, his eyes are clear, not clouded by confusion anymore. "What were you doing?"

I swallow. "You heard her. I was meeting someone." It comes out as a whisper. I've never told any serious lies before, and I'm not very good at it. And maybe it isn't a lie. I really was meeting someone.

"You weren't meeting anyone—at least not some boy. I know you better than that. Even if you were, you wouldn't have run from the guard unless it was important that you do so. I don't know how they couldn't see straight through your story, but I'm glad they didn't. I want you to tell me what's going on."

I stare at him, speechless. I never knew Dad paid so much attention to me. And I wrestle with what to say. Do I tell him about the chemo drugs? About Ava's brother? About the blinking lights? Fischer?

"Something strange is going on, Dad," I finally

say. "It's not the way I always thought it was."

"What do you me, 'something strange'?" His words are clipped. Impatient.

I watch his face, trying to gauge how much to say. Is he really going to believe me?

"I overheard the doctors talking about giving Mom chemo drugs. I didn't even know they had chemotherapy anymore, Dad. How could they not give it to her?"

"You shouldn't question their judgment, Hana. I still don't see how this relates to you sneaking out in the middle of the night. Who were you going to meet? Some group of backdoor chemotherapy salesmen?"

"Dad!"

"Well, who then? If you think you can explain, then I'm asking you to try."

"There are other strange things going on." I fumble for explanations that will make sense. "My friend, Ava, hasn't been allowed to see her brother for a week, and I saw blinking lights in the sky."

"Hana, you've got to stop this nonsense."

"You don't think this is important?" I ask.

"It doesn't matter if I think it's important. What matters is whether or not you trust the Greaters and their ability to take care of us. If they don't think she needs the chemo, then she probably doesn't. It also matters that we keep the law so we don't end up in some Lesser City. That means not breaking curfew, not entertaining anti-government thoughts, and not questioning the rules of our society." His voice rises and his face turns red.

"You don't think there are more important things than making the Greaters happy?" I demand. But one sentence sticks out to me: ...*so we don't end up in some*

Lesser city. Is that all that matters to him?

"You're young, Hana. You're going to have lots of passion for lots of things. Save it for your occupation. You can save the world then."

"Dad!" I can't stop the hot tears that burn my eyes. Why would he make fun of me for what I want to do with my life? As if I don't get that enough from kids at school.

"I'm giving you the truth, Hana. If you keep up this behavior, I'll turn you in myself. I won't let you ruin our family. Keep that in mind the next time you get it in your head to do something foolish."

He turns away from me, and I stare at him in utter dejection. Isn't he going to say anything? He's glad I'm OK? He loves me? Finally, I turn and head to the stairs.

"Hana."

I turn eagerly.

"Don't forget what I said."

19

My eyes feel like they've been rubbed with sand as I sit in class the next morning. I've never stayed up so late, and I can see why my parents have always wanted me in bed by ten. I never objected, mostly because there wasn't anything else to do.

"Hana? Are you OK?" Mrs. Sewell asks.

I glance up and realize she's standing right in front of me. Everyone in class stares at me in wide-eyed confusion.

"I asked if you could explain the basic order of the graduation service for everyone," she says. "But if you're not feeling well, then maybe you should see about going home." Her eyes are drawn together in worry.

"No, that's OK. I guess I'm just tired. I can do it."

Graduation is less than two weeks away now, and we've started practicing for the ceremony. A wave of excitement sweeps over me as I stand in front of the class, my tired body forgotten for the moment.

"The ceremony will be next Saturday at noon," I say. "We'll be seated in the gymnasium, and I'll give a speech. After the speech we'll be given our diplomas and a pamphlet that will help us prepare for our Tests the following Monday. That's it, in a nutshell."

"Thanks, Hana," Mrs. Sewell says. "Don't forget the graduation march, though. We're going to practice marching in and out next week."

Heat floods my face. "That's right."

She smiles and squeezes my shoulder. "You can go ahead and sit down. Does anyone have any questions about the pamphlet? I have a few to pass around, but you can't keep them until that night. The Greaters want your answers to be as fresh and honest as possible."

Paper shuffles as everyone passes the pamphlets around, and I take my seat.

My speech. I had forgotten all about it until I actually said the words. What am I going to say? I've been so busy with Mom, and then so confused because of Fischer and Jamie, I haven't had time to prepare. My stomach clenches at the thought of it.

I catch a glimpse of Lilith glaring at me from two seats up. What's her problem? She catches me looking and gives me one last glare before turning around.

Too bad she isn't the one giving the speech. At least it'd be funny, even if she didn't mean for it to be. Everyone would be laughing at her complete and utter self-absorption.

I can't imagine what I'll say to the kids preparing to take their Tests. *Be driven for your country! Follow the advice your Greater counselors give you, and you will succeed! Frost Moon promises happiness for all those under his care!* Lies, every one of them. Or at least that's what if feels like to me.

Regardless, I have to figure out what I'm going to say.

Mrs. Sewell heads to my desk when class is over. "Are you OK, Hana? You don't look yourself." Her eyes probe into mine.

"I'm fine, Mrs. Sewell. It's just been a long few weeks."

"How's your mom doing? Is she still in the hospital?"

"Yes, they say she can get better treatment there. I," I stop myself before I say I think it's ridiculous. That's probably not the best thing to go around saying. "I miss her."

Mrs. Sewell melts before my eyes. "I know you do, Hana. If you need some time, take it. You've been pulling quite a load at home, and here too."

"Thank you," I say. She smiles and retreats to her desk.

I grab my things and hurry from the classroom. Maybe I'll have a few minutes to work on my speech before I go to the hospital.

Lilith waits for me just outside, and her sour expression hasn't changed. "What's going on, Hana?"

"What are you talking about?" I slip my bag across my chest and keep walking. I'm tired, and I don't have time for her.

"I know something's going on with you, and Jamie too. You're not going to do something that's going to reflect badly on all of us are you?"

Reflect badly on all of us? What is she talking about? "Excuse me, Lilith," I say, stepping around her.

She grabs my arm, and I become as rigid as ice.

She doesn't let go. "I saw you out last night. You passed through my yard. Don't think I won't tell on you in a heartbeat." She releases my arm and stomps away.

I stare at her, open mouthed. How did she see me?

Her threat sends chills down my spine, mostly because I don't doubt she'll do what she says. But how does she know something's going on with Jamie? I glance around for my best friend and catch sight of her coming toward me. Her face gives me a hint of how Lilith or anyone else can make assumptions about her—it's red and puffy from crying.

"Jamie, are you OK?" I say.

"I don't feel so good. I haven't felt so good for a couple of days."

I have no idea what to say. Since I've never known anyone who was pregnant, I don't know if this is normal. "Come on to my house and relax," I say. So much for the speech.

She offers a weary smile. "Thanks, Hana. What would I do without you?"

I reach up to give her a quick squeeze, but inside my heart is bleeding. What will she do without me? She had better figure that out pretty quick, because soon she'll be on her own.

20

Jamie lies on my couch while I get her some water.

"I'm sorry I haven't been more supportive of your mom's sickness," she says. "I've been pretty selfish." Her face scrunches up and tears gather in her eyes again.

"Jamie, you've been as supportive as you could possibly be. I'm the one who kept insisting you not go to the hospital with me. Maybe if I would have been more supportive of you then you wouldn't be in this mess."

She shakes her head. "No, I think it happened before your mom even got sick."

"What?"

The sound of glass shattering rings around the tiny room. I hurry to clean up the mess I've made from dropping her water. "What do you mean, Jamie? We spent all of our time together before that."

"Not all of our time." She stands and tries to help pick up the glass.

"Go sit down, Jamie, before you cut yourself. If you have to go to the doctor they're going to find out you're pregnant." I don't know where my logic comes from, but she believes me and sits back down.

"What do you mean, though?" I ask. "We spent every minute of daylight together." I can't picture Jamie sneaking out in the dark, even though I've done it now.

She shakes her head. "Easton and I have the same free period at school."

My minds races back to the career fair, when they both disappeared. So that is the norm for them? My stomach clenches, and I feel like throwing up.

"Why didn't you ever mention all of this before?"

"Why would I? I knew what I was doing was wrong. Why involve you, too?"

I sigh in frustration. What am I supposed to say to that?

"I don't know what's going to happen to me, Hana. I'm scared to go to a Lesser city." She pulls her knees into her chest and rests her chin on them.

I want to say, *You should be!* But I don't. "It'll be scary, but you're tough. You're going to do well. I know it."

"Do you really believe that?"

"Of course I do." I give her a hug, and I notice that touching people is getting easier every time I do it. I suddenly want to open up to Jamie, to tell her everything that I've been going through. But where to start?

"Have you ever thought about God?"

I can tell by her wrinkled up nose that she thinks I'm being crazy. "What?"

"Have you ever thought about God? Do you think there is one?"

She sits on the edge of the couch now, frowning.

I dump the broken glass shards in the trash and sit beside her. "They outlawed religion because it separated the people. It caused wars and who knows what else. But what if the Greaters were wrong? What if there is a God, and that's why people fought— because some of them believed in Him, and others didn't?" I surprise even myself with this thought. I've been thinking of God on and off, but I didn't realize I'd put so much into it.

She stares at me open mouthed for a moment too long. I know she's not buying it. "What brought this on, Hana? Is it your mom's sickness? She's going to be OK, you know."

"No, it isn't that. Fischer says there are people around the city who believe it's true. I've just been thinking about it."

"Fischer again? I told you he was trouble. Unless you want to end up in a Lesser city like me then you should stay away from him. He's going to get you demoted for stirring rebellion."

I shiver at her words, because she's right. If I'm caught looking for religion it will be seen as rebellion against the society as a whole. I will definitely be demoted.

"I don't know, Jamie. I'm not taking it seriously." I think. "That's what we were going to meet for, though."

"Has that happened yet?" she asks.

"No. I tried to meet his group last night, but I was caught."

"What?" Her voice is an octave too high.

"A guard caught me and took me to the guard station. They asked what I was doing, and I told them I was meeting a boy."

Her eyes watch me wildly. "What did they say?"

"Not to do it again. They said it was my first strike, and if it happened three times I would be demoted."

"Hana, you have to stop!"

I laugh nervously. I don't want her to know how

scared I'm feeling. "What? You wouldn't want me as a neighbor in your next life?" I regret the words as soon as they're out. It's too terrible to joke about being a Lesser.

Her shoulders sag and she sits back against the couch. She starts crying again. "How do I prepare for something like this? I'll never see you again."

"You will, Jamie. I promise."

"You can't know that."

"No, but if I get my job in government I'll be able to travel to the communities I want to help. I'll find you." I have no idea if this is true, but I hope it is.

She stops her sniffling long enough to study me — to see if I mean it. Finally, she smiles. "I hope you do, Hana."

My dad walks through the door. He takes one look at Jamie's puffy face and freezes. "What happened?"

Jamie chuckles and stands up. "Just girl stuff, Mr. Norfolk. I was leaving, so don't worry about fixing my problems. Hana's on her way to the hospital, anyway."

I had almost forgotten about the hospital. I walk her to her door and give her one last hug. "I love you Jamie."

She smiles. "I know."

21

I push through the hospital doors, and as my eyes adjust, I see Ava lounging on one of the sofas in the lobby. I've never seen anyone sitting there in all the weeks since Mom's diagnosis. She smiles and jumps up to meet me. She seems completely at peace with the world.

It's such a change from the last time I saw her I can't help but ask, "Did you get to see Markus?"

"No," she says, that big smile still on her face.

"Oh. You just seem so happy, so I thought maybe—" I leave the sentence hanging.

"Well, I am feeling better. It just isn't because of Markus. I saw a doctor yesterday at the hospital. I kept crying and carrying on out in the hallway outside his door, and they took me aside. I told them my suspicions about Markus the night he got hurt. The doctor gave me the most wonderful medicine. It calmed my nerves and worries. I'm a little embarrassed now about my behavior. I just know things are going to be OK. I can't believe I made such a fool of myself."

Her words tumble out in a jumble, and I frown. "Wait, you told them?"

She nods.

A thousand questions run through my head. What kind of medicine did they give her? What did they say to her? But I only voice one. "Did you tell them you talked to me about it?"

She frowns and waves her hand dismissively. "No, there was no reason. They gave me the pills almost immediately."

Pills. "Did they tell you to meditate more?"

That's usually the Greaters' prescription for all mental woes. If we clear our minds and put our burdens off ourselves, we will feel better.

She shakes her head. "They said that meditation doesn't work for everyone, and that obviously it wasn't working for me. They said the pills would work."

I've never heard of anyone taking pills for their mind before. A few years ago, a neighbor of ours started acting strange. She kept ranting about bugs eating her skin, and she'd scratch until she bled. One day she just disappeared, and we all pretty much assumed she'd been sent to a Lesser city. She'd gone crazy and was no longer a productive member of society. Would medication have helped her?

This isn't like that. After all these years of hearing that meditation is the only way, I can't help but wonder why now? Why this introduction of pills to Ava?

And then it hits me. *To keep her quiet.* Markus' case is clearly different. Never before have I heard of anyone who wasn't allowed to see their loved one in the hospital. This all but confirms Ava's theory that her brother did more than fall from a tree. But if so, what? And why would Ava need pills to keep quiet about it?

"Did anyone else in your family get the pills?"

Ava shakes her head. "No, my dad's OK. My mom refused them. I'm working on that, though. They will really help her feel better."

We reach the stairwell and climb quietly to our floors.

"I'll see you around, Hana."

I wave as she steps through the door. It slams shut behind her. I stare at the cold metal, thinking about what she said. She took her concerns to someone who could help—a doctor, and therefore a Greater—and instead of a solution to the problem, she was given a pill. Chills creep up my spine at the implications. A pill to shut her up, because they didn't want her asking questions or trying to figure things out. I'm more convinced than ever that something is going on with Markus.

Ava obviously doesn't see any need to explore the situation further. That bothers me.

Fischer is in Mom's room when I get there. She's sleeping.

"Don't you ever get a day off?" I ask. I'm trying to lighten the mood, but I'm anxious to hear how last night went for him. Did they wait for me? Did they know why I never came?

He smiles, and I'm surprised that he doesn't appear to have had a single worry about me. "It's part of the training. You'd better get used to it now."

"Really? You don't get a day off?" No wonder Keegan doesn't have time to write.

"We get a day here and there, but I don't mind. This is what I want to do. How much longer until your Test, again?"

"About two weeks." I can't believe it's coming so fast. I've been so confused lately I just hope I don't end up as Lesser at the end of it all.

"You'll do great," Fischer says.

Did he read my mind?

I glance at Mom and frown a little. "Can I ask you a question?"

His lighthearted face changes immediately and he's all ears. "Absolutely. What do you need?"

I bite my lip and take a cautionary look at the door. "Do you know anything about pills? Like for people who can't calm down through meditation?"

He smiles a sad, lopsided smile. "Unfortunately, yes. Why do you ask?"

I hug my arms to my stomach. "They've given some to my friend, Ava, because she wouldn't calm down about her brother. That's—that's another strange thing. They won't let the family see him."

He watches my face for what seems like forever. Finally, he nods slowly. "I'm not surprised, but I'll see what I can find out."

I smile a little. "Thanks, Fischer. How do you know about the pills?"

"They give them to Lessers all the time."

Of course. The Lessers aren't strong enough to do anything on their own, are they? All the more reason they need help.

He frowns a little, watching my face, but finally he asks, "Did you sleep well?"

I lick my lips. "Not particularly. We had visitors."

"I heard."

Does he mean he literally heard the chase? But I don't ask.

He goes to the door and glances out. "It's my fault, and I'm sorry. I should have known something like that wasn't the best idea."

I shake my head. "No, it's not your fault. I'm the one who wasn't paying attention."

Fischer smiles like he always does, dropping the subject and letting me win. "We'll figure something out, and soon. I'll let you know." He slips into the hall.

After my visit with Mom, I go back home. I make it well before curfew this time. My dad sits grading tests at the kitchen counter.

"There's another letter for you." He nods toward a white envelope beside the sink.

No hi, or how was your day. He's still upset from last night.

I snatch it up and head for the stairs. I never wrote Keegan back after his last letter. I just figured he was obviously too busy, and he didn't have time to read about the strange things going on around here. Besides that, I really didn't think about him all that much.

I roll out my meditation mat and flip off my shoes. Meditation might not work for Ava, but it does make *me* feel better. Maybe that's why I'm so edgy, because I haven't meditated in so long. I settle onto the mat and rip the letter open.

Dear Hana, I'm sorry for the short letter last time. It has been so busy around here. We actually went on a trip to Greater City. Greater City! *Can you believe it? It was crazy there. There are strange cars, and they have these places called movie theaters. A movie is like a play, but it's on a screen. The people aren't really there. I guess that sounds weird, but you'd have to see it to understand.*

He's right. It does sound really weird. I frown at the thought of all the Greaters having cars, though. I thought there wasn't enough gas to go around. I don't understand why everyone there gets to use it up.

If you get to work in government, you'll get to come, too, Hana. They say the government studies come here often. You'll love it!

We came to meet the important people in the entertainment industry. They think I'll do best in music, since I sing and play guitar.

He sings and plays very well. He's mesmerized me more than once.

I'm going to be home in two weeks. Isn't that great? I'll be there when you take your Test. You're going to do great. I can't wait to see you. Keegan.

He sounds happy and truly excited to come home. I try and put Greater City out of my mind so I can meditate, but I'm not very successful. I keep picturing movies on a screen, where the actors are taking odd pills to calm their nerves.

22

My shoes make a soft thud with each step I take toward Ava's house. It's Sunday morning and Dad went to the hospital to visit Mom. I've decided that if Ava isn't going to figure out what Markus was doing that night, I'm going to try.

Maybe it will help sharpen my sneaking skills too, since I'm going to try and do this without drawing any attention to myself, and I definitely plan on meeting Fischer again. I'm curious about the address he gave me on Kensington Avenue. What would I have found if I'd met him? If I do well here, I might sneak over there, too.

A few kids play in their yards on Ava's street. Houses are lined up like dominoes down the old pavement, and I hurry toward Ava's. It looks like the house is empty, but really, how could I tell?

Taking care to avoid the front windows, I sneak to the side of the house where I know Ava's room is. It's most likely that Markus climbed out this window when he sneaked out of his house that night.

It strikes me that he sneaked out. I always thought of people sneaking out for one reason—to meet a boy or girl. Now I realize there are other reasons. After all, I sneaked out to meet Fischer's group. Really, there are endless possibilities. Maybe there are people who cause trouble at night. Rob people. Murder people. We've always been told that all crime happens by the

Lessers, but really, how would we know that's true? We're all inside when the crimes happen.

There's a tree right outside Ava's window. That gives me pause. If Markus was trying to get out of his window, he would have certainly used this tree. He could have fallen from it easily, no questions asked. In that case, it wouldn't matter why he was sneaking out, just that he was, and that he'd fallen from the tree in the process.

My resolve waivers. Maybe it is as everyone says—he fell from a tree.

This isn't going to be as easy as I thought.

I force my mind to go through the possibilities. If he had simply fallen from a tree, would they keep him locked up? Would they refuse to let the family see him?

No.

I push forward. He obviously didn't fall from this tree, or else they wouldn't have known what he was up to. I need to figure out where Markus went from here. I look up and down the alley between houses. One path leads further into the city. The other path leads toward the levies.

If he was meeting a girl, he would probably head toward the levy. If he was meeting a group like Fischer's, he would probably head toward the city.

I try to remember Markus from school. Does he seem the type to meet in a clandestine group, discussing a rebellion?

That thought almost stops me. A rebellion? Is that what Fischer is doing? Is that what I want?

I go back to the task at hand. I didn't know Markus well, but he doesn't seem the type. Then again, does Fischer? Do I?

I choose the 'meeting a girl' angle and head toward the levy. The path is a clearly defined dirt track, a lot like the one near my house. It takes much longer to get through the trees and reach the levies, though, and I'm surprised when I come out at the same place as the path that starts on my street.

My eyes immediately find the broken tree limbs and beaten down grass patches I noticed last week. I gasp. This is where Markus fell.

What did he see from that tree?

I look into the distance. No blinking lights greet me this day. Whatever they were, they're gone now. Did Markus see them? Did they draw him here? Is that what made him fall from his tree?

My breaths come in short, shallow puffs. I've just made a major discovery, but it gives me chills. If they locked him up for seeing the lights then it's good that I didn't get caught as well. I'm glad I didn't tell anyone.

I head back toward the city. As crazy as it is, I still want to see Kensington Avenue. I've been thinking the past couple of days that I hope I didn't get anyone in trouble. I don't think Fischer would tell me if I had. He's too nice, and he wouldn't want me to feel guilty. Did the guards go looking for the 'boy' I was supposed to meet? Did they find Fischer's group?

I doubt it, since Fischer was at the hospital yesterday, but I want to see the place for myself.

I don't worry about sneaking anymore. It's broad daylight, and no one is paying attention to me anyway. I slow down as I reach the older parts of town, though. It might look strange, me going in there by myself. It's not like it's a well-travelled part of town. I look around, and when I don't see anyone, I move forward. I won't get this chance again for an entire week—the last break before my Test—and I don't want my resolve to fade.

An acrid smell hangs in the air, and I realize it's not just the smell, it's actually the air. It's thick, and it stinks. I put my sleeve to my nose and continue walking. Ash blows past me with the wind.

The old houses look better and worse in the light. Better because they're not so foreboding, but worse because I can see how very dilapidated they are. Now that I'm not really trying to sneak and hurry through the night, I actually get to Kensington Avenue quickly. I hurry to the place I got caught, and then start looking at house numbers from there. I get to 871 and freeze.

The house is not there, because it's been burned to the ground.

23

I glance around in a panic. No one is waiting for me. No one is watching my reaction. Still, I can't shake that trapped feeling, the feeling someone is watching me. I feel stark and naked and exposed, like I'm standing in an open field just waiting to be speared by the hunter.

I hurry toward home, glancing ahead and around and behind me constantly. I don't see a single person who seems to be paying me any attention as I pass through street after street, but I feel much better once I've gone into my own house and closed the door behind me.

My breath comes in short puffs. In, out, in, out. No one is following me. If they had been, wouldn't they have stopped me before I got out of the old neighborhoods? I have no idea, but I can't get home fast enough. Once I get inside I do something I've never done before. I lock the door.

A shudder races through me, and I grab a blanket and curl up on the couch. I usually wait for Dad to get home from the hospital before I head there, but today I'm thinking of going now. My parents and I haven't been together in so long it feels like eternity.

That makes my decision for me.

The walk to the hospital is scary. Empty buildings tower over me with every step. Shadows hide spies and guards, and maybe Lessers who wait to rob me.

I know I'm being ridiculous, but I can't help it.

The familiar lamps in the hospital lobby welcome me. Their warm glow isn't confusing anymore. Instead, it's comforting. I fly up the stairs to the third floor.

Dr. Bentford is on duty today, dressed in a crisp, white lab coat. He smiles as he passes me in the hall. "Hi, Miss Norfolk. How are you today?"

My heart still races out of fear, but I already feel much calmer. "I'm fine," I say to the doctor who wanted to refuse Mom her chemotherapy drugs.

Fischer comes from behind a door carrying two glasses of water. "Hana! I was just taking these to your parents." He pauses when he takes in my appearance. "Are you OK? Would you like a glass?"

"That's OK. I just didn't want to be home by myself." Can I explain why? It's probably best not to, at least not here.

Like he always does, Fischer seems to sense I want to say more than what I am. "I get a break in a little while. You're welcome to join me on the roof."

"That would be great. Do you want me to take the water?" I reach out, but he shakes his head.

"That's OK. I'll walk with you."

We walk in silence to Mom's room, but I'm glad for the company. My nerves are calming now. I push through the door and freeze. My dad sits beside Mom's bed, holding her hand. I haven't seen my parents together in so long unexpected tears burn my eyes. I miss my family. I miss my regular life. I miss the way things used to be.

"Hana," Mom says. She notices my tears right away, and of course, she knows why I'm crying. She holds her arms out to me, and I rush into them. We hug each other like we haven't done in years, and in less than a minute we're all crying.

When I look up, the water glasses are on the bedside table and Fischer has disappeared.

"Why did you come so early?" Dad asks.

"I didn't want to be alone. It seemed like a good idea for us all to be together."

"It *was* a good idea. Why haven't we realized this before?" Mom says.

I take a shuddering breath and shrug. "I think we wanted to make sure you spent as little time as possible by yourself. So Dad came for part of the day, and I came for the other part."

Mom nods. "That makes sense, but from now on let's do it this way, at least sometimes."

"Deal," I say.

My dad nods his approval.

I notice now how Mom looks. She's skinny—no not just skinny, she's frail. I feel like hugging her too tightly will break her. I wonder if she coughs whether she'll snap in half.

"Are you eating the fruits and vegetables, Mom? You've lost weight."

She waves her hand like it doesn't matter, but I know it does. "I haven't been hungry lately. I never do anything exhausting. I only lay here all day."

I have other questions, but I don't want to upset her. Can she even walk? Does she hurt? Or does she spend most days on pain medicine?

Then I wonder about the pills Ava takes. Do they give them to Mom, to help her deal with her illness? More questions I don't ask.

Fischer will probably know the answer about the pills. I'll ask him when I meet him on the roof.

A few minutes pass and I excuse myself to the

bathroom. Since I don't want to lie, I go ahead and head to the restroom before going upstairs and outside.

Being outdoors doesn't intimidate me when I'm above the city. Warm rays of sun beat down on my arms, and a light breeze pushes my hair from my face. I close my eyes and take a deep breath. No one is waiting for me here, waiting to arrest me.

Fischer's eyes stare back at me when I open my eyes. The look on his face is intense. "I'm glad you're OK. I was worried when I saw you drive away with the guards."

My ears burn, and I quickly look away. "I wondered if you knew what happened."

Some strange electricity hangs in the air between us, and I don't know what to say.

Finally, he clears his throat. "It must be good to have your whole family together again." I know he's a true medic—a servant. He really wants to help people, to make them feel better. In that moment I'm convinced the system works. The Test really does determine who your best you is.

"It feels better than anything," I say. "You can't imagine how hard it is to be separated with no choice."

His eyes flash with—pain? He pats the concrete beside him. "Sit."

I lower myself onto the hot concrete ledge. "Will you go back to your family when you finish your training?"

"No. I'll probably stay here." The way he says it is so unlike Fischer's normal way of talking. It's short and to the point, almost snappy. I don't ask him anything else.

Fischer takes a bite of his sandwich and looks out over the city. Buildings rise and fall all over the horizon, for as far as the eye can see. Most of them aren't even used and are falling apart in disrepair. Who used to live in them, and what happened to those people?

He offers me part of his sandwich, but I shake my head.

"You looked upset today. Is that why you came?" This sounds more like the Fischer I know. More willing to talk about others than him.

I take a deep breath and look at my hands, wondering how he reads me so well. "I went to Kensington Avenue. The house was burned down. I just couldn't figure who burned it down, and why. It gave me the creeps."

He watches me speak, nodding his understanding. When I finish he looks back to the city. "I'm not surprised."

When he doesn't go on I say, "So who burned it down?"

"My guess is the Greaters."

"Would they do that?" I ask in a small voice.

He sighs and finally turns back to me. "Yes, and more, if they suspect someone was meeting there. Do you still want to meet with the others?"

"Yes," I say without hesitation. "I think Ava's brother saw something, or maybe he did something. That's what got him put in confinement. I want to know more about that, and about chemo drugs, pills, and flashing lights in the sky."

Fischer frowns. "What did you say?"

I forgot I hadn't mentioned those to anyone yet. I shrug. "I saw flashing lights in the sky, out past the levies."

"When?"

"It's been almost two weeks. The last time it rained."

"It sounds like lightning."

I shake my head. "It was definitely not lightning. Trust me."

He takes me seriously, but obviously doesn't have an answer for me. "I tried to find out exactly what's wrong with Ava's brother, but they have his files sealed tight. That in itself tells me something fishy is going on, but you may be right about the lights. Markus had met with our group once, him and his friend. They mentioned seeing them."

I'm shocked speechless. Finally, I sputter and say, "Why didn't you tell me that before?"

He shrugs. "Secrets are important when you're going against the government. I didn't see why I needed to mention it until now." His words are soft, honest, raw.

I understand completely. "So when can we meet?" The words come out wrong, and my cheeks burn. I hope he doesn't take it like I think we're meeting just the two of us.

Fischer pretends not to notice how awkward things feel. "I think it's better if we just do things out in the open, instead of trying to sneak around. Meet somewhere ordinary. The others agree."

"Won't a group draw more attention?"

He shakes his head. "There won't be a group."

I clear my throat and look away, Jamie's warnings coming back to me, and I realize I wasn't so far off in what I said a minute ago. "So when should I meet you? I thought you never got a day off."

"I don't," he says with a smile. "You won't be meeting me. He'll be in the food market tomorrow.

He's short, with hair like honey—that deep golden red color. You'll know him. His name is Mr. Elders."

My cheeks flame an even hotter shade of red. That's the second time I've assumed he would be meeting me alone. "Won't the market be dangerous? There are so many people around."

"Trust me, Hana."

The way he says it, and the humble yet confident look on his face, puts me at ease. I do trust him.

"OK. I'll be there." I need to return to Mom's room, but before I go I have one last question. "Fischer?" Saying his name feels funny on my tongue. Good funny. "Do you think they know why I was out the other night? Is that why they burned down the house?"

"I don't know," he says right away. "I have to say no, because they wouldn't let you go so easily. On the other hand, how did they know to burn it down? I was the only one there. I was supposed to meet you and bring you to the meeting place. I didn't leave any evidence behind." He shakes his head. "I just don't know."

I swallow around the ball in my throat, and my hands feel cold and clammy. "Do you think they're following me?" This is my real fear, that they're going to take me off the street and lock me up. Or worse, make me a mindless citizen, mellowed out on pills like Ava.

He smiles his reassuring smile, the one that has put me at ease since I first met him. "I don't think so. Even if they do suspect you, they'll watch to see if you're part of a rebellion before they do anything about it. They won't bother you, at least not until you give them proof."

His words surprise me. I want to ask him if that's what he's a part of—a rebellion. And I want to ask him what happened to make him want to rebel.

"You're taking chances by talking to me, aren't you?" I ask.

He shrugs noncommittally. "I don't think so. They're not paying me any more attention now than they were before."

Again I want to ask him more, like how he knows how much they watch him. I move to sit back down but he stops me.

"I have to get back downstairs. You should do the same."

I pause mid sit, fighting the sting his words bring, but then I straighten and nod. "Right. Thanks for talking to me, Fischer."

"Tomorrow in the market," he says. "Don't forget."

24

My mom and dad have barely noticed I was gone. They miss each other, and this makes me sad. Their heads are bent close, and they're holding hands. It takes a moment for them to notice me standing at the door.

"Did you find the bathroom?" Dad asks. He pulls back from Mom but keeps hold of her hand.

That he thinks I don't know where the bathroom is strikes me as funny and I laugh. "Yes Dad. I've been coming here almost every day for two weeks now. I've used the bathroom more than once."

He smiles ruefully. "That's true." He seems lighthearted for the first time in a long time, and I'm glad to see him this way.

I wonder then if he told Mom about the guard bringing me home in the middle of the night. I doubt it, since he wouldn't want to upset her. I silently thank him for that. The last thing she needs is to worry about me, and at least it looks like he's forgiven me.

Mom reaches her hand out, beckoning me. "Come sit by me."

I sit in the small chair beside her bed and take her other hand.

"I need to remember this moment," Mom says.

The shock of her statement hits me like a punch in the gut. "Don't say that, Mom. We'll have more times together."

"What?" she says. "Don't I have the right to remember my favorite moments?"

I hate what she's saying. I don't want this to be her favorite moment. It's definitely not mine. Then I realize maybe it is. Maybe it's one of my favorite moments in the last few weeks, the weeks since her diagnosis.

"I've read one of the books you brought," she says. "I really liked it."

This is a safe subject. Mom must know I don't want to talk about sentimental things. I smile. "I'm glad, Mom. I can bring you more. In fact, I think I want to go to the market tomorrow. Do you want me to pick something for you?"

Now I've set the stage for my absence tomorrow and for my trip to the market. It won't come as a surprise, and I'll be able to meet Fischer's man.

"No, save your allowance for yourself. I don't need anything in this place. I think Fischer would get me a book if I wanted one anyway."

"Could he really do that?" What else does Fischer have access to?

My mom smiles wearily. "I have no idea what resources are available to him, but he's never denied a single request I've made."

I listen closely to her words and a warm liquid fills my bones. I admire Fischer for all he does. Unfortunately, though, there is one thing she needs which Fischer can't get her, not yet, anyway. The chemo. Will Fischer tell me when the request is answered? This is something I need to ask him, and soon.

"Fine, I'll save the allowance for me. What should I buy?"

"Whatever your heart desires, Hana," Mom says.

"I want you to have everything you want."

I don't tell her, but that's nearly impossible. What I want is the last three weeks to have never happened. I want the mutation to go away and her to come home. I want to have never heard about chemo drugs, or corrupt government. I want my best friend to not be pregnant.

I hold in my tears and smile instead. I hug her tightly. "Thanks, Mom."

"What's that hug for?"

"Just because," I say with a nervous laugh. I can't hold my tears anymore, and I'm embarrassed to cry in front of them again.

My mom pulls my head to her chest and strokes my short hair. "It'll be OK," she whispers.

If only I could believe her.

My dad and I stay until just before curfew, and we walk home together. I'm thankful for this because despite Fischer's words, I'm not convinced someone isn't watching me. I can't keep the tears at bay, no matter how hard I try.

"Don't worry about supper," Dad says when we get home. "We can find something simple to eat."

I wipe the tears from my face and try to smile. "Thanks, Dad."

A loud rap beats at the door and I jump.

My dad frowns. "I'll get it."

I watch him go to the door. Should I hide in the small pantry? What if it's a guard coming to take me away?

"Can I talk to Hana?"

It's Jamie's voice, and she's upset. I push past Dad.

"What's wrong?" I ask. She's crying and she comes inside and shuts the door.

"They're coming for me."

"What?" But I'm pretty sure I already know who she's talking about.

Her gaze darts around frantically. "They're coming for me. Tonight."

"Jamie, are you in trouble?" Dad asks. "Do your parents know what's going on?"

"I told them," she says to me. "My mom went crazy. She said she was going to drag me to the hospital herself. I told her that I wasn't having an abortion no matter what. She was furious and went to the guard station. They're coming for me." She starts sobbing uncontrollably and I pull her into a hug.

My dad stands there like a statue, his face frozen in what must be shock.

"Is your dad home?" I ask.

She shakes her head. "He is now, but he wasn't then. I told him what happened and he didn't say anything. He just stared at me, and then he went to his room and shut the door."

"Have you talked to Easton anymore?"

"Yes! He said he would marry me. He said he didn't care if they make us Lessers."

My eyes burn and I blink away the tears. If they're coming for her now, then this will be the last time I see her. My brain rebels. "You have to hide, Jamie."

She's crying harder and shaking her head. "Where?" she says. "Where would I go? They won't give me food allowance or electricity allowance. They won't give me anything if I don't cooperate. I have to take care of my baby."

My dad finally snaps out of his shock. "You're right, Jamie. You need to cooperate with them. And listen to them. You don't want to become a Lesser.

Your baby won't last in that kind of atmosphere."

I whip around to Dad in shock. My head spins and I stare at him open mouthed. "Are you saying she should murder her baby?"

He frowns and shakes his head. "Stop being so dramatic, Hana. There will be time later for babies."

I feel like my body is as red as a lobster. Anger boils up and out of my mouth like lava from a volcano. "How dare you! You're as corrupt and horrible as they are!" I take Jamie by the shoulders. "If you won't run then you have to stand your ground. Do you hear me, Jamie?"

She nods, still crying, but her face doesn't look all that determined to put up a fight.

"They'll bring Easton in, too. You have to stick up for yourself, even if Easton changes his mind. Can you do this even if he can't?" It's something to consider. Easton might put on a brave front for her, but when he's truthfully faced with becoming a Lesser, what will he do then?

"He won't change his mind," she says. Her eyes look surer of this statement.

"But if he does, Jamie…" My emotions race out of control, and I stop to rein them in. "Jamie, he might. If he does, you have to stand firm."

Finally, she nods. "I know. I will."

We stare into each other's eyes for what seems like forever. "You're my best friend," she says.

"And you're mine!" I say. I wrap her in the tightest hug I've ever given.

"What if I never see you again?" she asks.

I swallow hard. "I'll do what I can," I say. I'm more determined than ever to pass my Test in two weeks. "I will see you again, Jamie. I will."

We hear them outside then, only they're not outside my house but Jamie's. We all look at the front door, knowing it's only going to take a few minutes for them to look here.

My dad steps forward and wraps Jamie in a hug. "Stay away from alcohol and the pills," he says. "That's how they get you."

I whip my head toward him and stare in shock. He knows about the pills? What else does he know about? God?

I can tell by Jamie's expression that she doesn't register what he said, but I am shocked by it. My dad must know more than he lets on, or maybe it's more than he wants to believe. I've heard of people living in denial. Maybe that's what he's doing.

The guards bang on our door, and Jamie stiffens in my arms as Dad answers it.

"We're looking for Jamie Stanlin," a guard says. "Is she here?"

My dad pauses only a moment before stepping away from the door to let the guards enter.

"Jamie Stanlin?"

Jamie sniffles and nods.

The guard takes her arm gently. "If you'll come with us, Miss Stanlin, we have some things to discuss."

I watch my best friend walk from my front door for the last time. "Jamie!" I cry, throwing myself at her. We hug one last time, and then I let her go.

The guards load her into their car, and Jamie disappears from my street forever.

25

My mind spins all night long. They've taken Jamie away. What's to keep them from taking me? My mom? Markus? Any of us? I lay in bed wide awake, and when the sun peeks through my window I know it's OK to get ready for school.

I want to make sure I'm there on time. In fact, I want to make sure I do everything exactly right. If I don't, they might take me.

I feel dead as I walk to school. I don't notice anyone else on their way to school or work, even though I'm sure the others are there. I'm just blind and deaf and dumb.

School looks the same as always. I'm not sure if I expected everyone to be mourning Jamie's demotion or not. Most of them probably haven't even heard yet. That won't last, though.

I can't help it; I scan the hallways for Easton. Did they take him, too? Did they drag him from his parents, from his home? I don't see him, and so I assume he kept his promise to Jamie. That's something, at least.

The students buzz because it's the last week of school. There is so much to do, and everyone rushes through the halls. Someone bumps me.

"Oh, excuse me," he says.

I don't reply and he frowns, but then he hurries away.

It isn't long into the morning when I hear the first whispers. Graham Miller leans across the aisle in math class and whispers to Lilith, "Did you hear about Jamie Stanlin? She got pregnant."

They both turn and look at me, and even Lilith has the good sense to quickly turn back to the front.

My stomach burns. What's happening to Jamie right now? Is she already in a Lesser city, or are they still trying to make her change her mind? What if they didn't even give her a choice? That thought makes my stomach turn, because I realize it's a possibility.

By the end of the school day, people are avoiding me. They don't want to bump into me, or risk having to speak to me. I'm awkward now. I'm dangerous. I'm associated with Jamie—someone who's been demoted. Even Mrs. Sewell doesn't say much, other than, "Do you have your speech ready for Saturday?"

Lilith watches me all day. Not with a scowl or hatred. Just with interest. It's disconcerting.

Finally, school is out. All at once, my spirits lift. I'm going to the market, and I'm going to meet someone who can shed light on the strange things happening in our city. I've been so lifeless all day, so afraid of getting in trouble. I'm ready to be alive again. I make myself walk to the market place at a normal pace. It would look suspicious if I were spotted running through the streets.

The market place isn't as crowded today. That's bad for me, I realize. If the place is crawling with people, it's less likely anyone will notice me talking to one particular person. But if it's empty, there's no way to be inconspicuous.

The man with honey-colored hair isn't at the market yet. I pretend to look at fruit and vegetables while I wait. I scan the crowd for Easton's table, but he isn't here, either. Proof that they took him, too.

"Aren't you keeping your garden anymore?" a vendor asks.

I smile tightly at the short man. Of course, he would recognize my behavior as odd. I've been coming to the market place for years, and never have I bought produce. "I just wanted to see how the crops turned out compared to ours. Our last batch of tomatoes didn't turn out too well." At least I'm not lying. His tomatoes are plump and red, while ours were small and hard.

The man's bushy eyebrows fly up. "Tomatoes? Why, that's the easiest crop there is. Are they getting enough sun?"

"They're in the full sun," I say. "We just haven't been home very much lately to tend them." I hope he doesn't ask why, because I don't want to explain about Mom.

He doesn't, he just smiles and nods knowingly.

I turn to move along, and that's when I spot him. The man with honey-colored hair is browsing the fruit stand a few feet from me. I wonder how I should approach him, but he doesn't even acknowledge me.

"Excuse me," he says, bumping around me. He continues browsing, buying a huge armful of produce.

What's his plan?

I meander through the stands, until I'm standing on the outskirts. Waiting. Sweat beads on my back. I don't know if it's from the hot sun or my nerves.

The man buys his fruit and looks like he's leaving.

Maybe this isn't the man Fischer sent. Maybe I was wrong and I should be looking for someone else altogether. I scan the small crowd, but there's no one else who meets the criteria.

One thing's for sure—I have to keep moving. Standing in the middle of the market will look suspicious all by itself.

Umph!

"Oh, excuse me, miss," someone grunts. It's Mr. Elders, the honey-haired man.

A bag of fruit lays spilled over the pavement.

"Will you help me pick these up?" he asks.

I bend without thinking and start scooping fruit into my arms.

"More slowly, please," he says softly. He goes on whispering, as if we were already in conversation. "The chemo is only for the Greaters. Your mom never had a shot at getting it, and her doctor was taking a big risk even applying. It's expensive, and they're not going to spend that money on anyone other than the most important."

My stomach flips. What is he saying? Has her chemo been denied? "But we're not Lessers. I don't understand," I stutter.

A smile plays on his thin lips. "We're all Lessers, unless we're Greaters. And even some of them are Lessers."

I think back over the last two weeks. All of the strange things that have happened seem to confirm his statement. No one is all that important. Not Ava's family, or mine, or Jamie's. "Why?"

"They save things like chemo for the Greaters. They don't want to die of the mutation or anything else if they can help it, but chemo and other medications are expensive. They save them for the ones who are important, and who are rich enough to pay for them. The Greaters are the ones who possess the greatest ability to make decisions, to lie, and to lead, or so they think. The Greaters need each other. If the people of our country trust in anyone else, then the Greaters' power will be no more. That's why we can't even have a god."

He's speaking so fast, while his arms move so slowly at gathering his purchases. His words jumble together and I have to concentrate to figure out exactly what he's saying.

"A god?" I ask. That's what Fischer said on the hospital roof. He talked about God, too. I'm not sure I see the connection. What does denying God have to do with the Greaters?

"I don't understand," I finally say. I'm working to keep my face neutral, because inside my body is shriveling like a raisin. My mom's chemotherapy drugs were denied, and no one told me. Fischer didn't tell me.

I pick up the final piece of fruit and place it in his bundle. We both rise. Only a minute has passed, but it already feels like we've attracted too much attention.

"Thank you, miss," he says loudly. "I would appreciate that help getting these home."

I take the hint and relieve him from some of his burden. "It's no problem," I say, smiling. We leave together, and I can't help glancing behind me to make sure no one is watching.

I see a flash of a shadow as someone turns a corner. Is it a guard following me?

We walk a few moments in silence, when finally he speaks. "Do you know about God?"

I rack my brain, trying to remember the bits and pieces of things I've heard in the past. "The people in the Early Days believed in some kind of God, right? He made the world or something, and He takes care of people when they die." That last part is just something I came up with on my own, based on the argument my parents had all those years ago.

He nods. "He *did* make the world, and He made us—you and me. The Greaters took him away long ago, for a reason. If people trust in a God, they won't trust in the Greaters. The people must rely on them to supply their needs. If they're trusting God to take care of them in life and death, what do they need the Greaters for?"

His words sink in, and I wonder if they're true. If God is in control, then maybe He *is* the one who controls where we go when we die.

We round a corner, and immediately I see him. A guard, coming down the sidewalk toward us.

My heart stutters in my chest cavity. What if he heard the honey-haired man? What if he's coming for us?

"Thank you, miss. This is my house. I really appreciate your help." He takes the fruit from my arms and walks through the gate to the house.

The guard smiles at me as he passes. I keep walking, too, even though I didn't pay attention to where we went, and I don't know how to get home. The pounding of my heart slows down when I'm sure the guard has turned the corner and is out of sight. He's not going to stop me and ask for ID. He's not going to ask me what I was doing with that man. He's not going to ask what we were talking about.

I pause on the shady sidewalk and glance around. Nothing looks familiar, and there are rows and rows of houses. I don't know which way takes me home, but I can try and retrace my steps.

The honey-haired man is gone, even though I'm sure that wasn't his house he walked toward. I pass the house and continue on.

My head continues its spinning from yesterday. A God? Can it be true? *Is* there a Being in the sky Who created the world?

It seems Fischer believes it. I try to remember exactly what he'd said that day on the roof. He'd said there was Someone I could put my trust in. That's what Mr. Elders said, too. We could trust in God to take care of us, which is why the Greaters didn't want him around. I'm confused by the references and connections.

The man had said the Greaters needed more Greaters. They were the smart ones, the powerful ones, the ones who were good at making decisions.

That makes me wonder why they even need the Middles and Lessers around, but then the answer seems obvious. They can't be rulers without someone to rule.

My stomach churns. Mom means nothing to them. They don't care enough about her to even try and save her life. They have a lifeline, and they're not willing to throw it to her.

I round the corner heading back toward the market place. Or at least I hope I'm heading that way. My steps pick up speed as my anger grows. It isn't fair. Why do we let this go on? Why does Dad let it go on? It's obvious he knows about the corruption. He told Jamie to stay away from the pills. Were they the same pills the doctors gave Ava? It's most likely they are.

My dad knows about the pills. What else does he know about? God?

My brain tells me the whole 'God' thing is a joke.

There is no God. How could there be? Does He just sit up in the sky and watch us here on earth, while we starve and fight for our lives? Why doesn't He do something? Why doesn't He stop the evil?

But my heart tells me it's true. It tells me everything Mr. Elders told me is true, and that I'm missing important information.

There have to be answers somewhere. There have to be, and I'm going to find them.

26

Once I'm back at the market I pause. Where should I go? Before I can change my mind, I head toward the hospital. I want to know if what Mr. Elders said about Mom's chemo is true. Has it been denied? I want to know why Fischer told this man and didn't tell me, and I want to know now.

I charge up the steps two at a time and push through the heavy metal door onto the third floor.

Dr. Lane smiles at me in the hallway, but I don't return the kindness. Instead, I head straight to Fischer, my heart doing double time. "Tell me about the chemo," I say.

He frowns, glancing around. "What are you talking about?"

I glance around, too, and Dr. Lane has disappeared. We're alone in the hallway. "Mr. Elders said the chemo was denied. Is it true?"

He watches me for a full minute. Finally, he looks down. "Yes. It happened yesterday."

"Before you saw me, or after?"

He doesn't look up. "Before."

The breath goes out of me in a rush. I try and gulp in more, but nothing comes. Am I suffocating? Is this what it feels like to die?

Finally, I pull in a breath, but I suck in too much. I cough and sputter, and Fischer comes around his desk to pat my back. It's something Mom used to do when I was little. An odd comfort spreads over me.

"Why didn't you tell me?" I ask, tears filling my eyes.

He looks up at me with a sad, sorrowful face. "I just couldn't. I'm sorry."

I shake my head, stepping away from him. "I don't understand why you would keep it from me. Were you ever planning on telling me?"

"Yes. It's all I've thought of since I saw it in her chart." He stops talking again, glancing around like he's just realized he said way too much right out in the open. He steps closer to me. "Listen, we can talk more, later. For now, this isn't safe. But please believe me when I say I'm sorry. Very, very sorry."

He looks sincere, but I'm still mad at him. "Fine." I swipe at the tears on my cheeks. "But we are going to talk more, later. We are."

"I swear."

I think about going to Mom's room now, but Dad's with her. My eyes are wet with tears, and my heart hasn't slowed down. I don't want to be questioned about my day, or why I'm not at the market, so instead I head home.

My eyes dart around the street, constantly scanning for shadows and movement. I can't shake the feeling I'm being followed. It's irrational, I know, and I wonder if I'll ever feel normal again. Still, I can't help but feel relief when I step into my own house. I stare at the lock, willing myself not to turn it.

My fear wins out as I reach forward and twist it into place. It brings the strangest sense of comfort.

I tinker around the living room for a while, and then head upstairs to clean my bedroom. Everything Mr. Elders said runs through my mind. A God. More

Greaters. No chemo.

My anger sparks again at the thought. What gives them the right to choose who lives and who dies? Why should they get to decide who should be Greater, Middle, or Lesser?

Jamie isn't violent or a drain on society. Is she? Is she putting a burden on society just by having a baby if she is going to continue working, as would Easton? What she did was wrong, I know, but I'm angry that she had to be sent away just because she wouldn't kill her own baby.

Every law we have races through my mind, and I question them all.

Why would God let this happen?

Then again, how did the people let this happen? Why didn't anyone fight against it? Is there more to the story?

I'm so wrapped up in my thoughts that I jump when I hear someone banging on the front door.

"Hana? Are you in there?" Dad's voice drifts up to me.

I forgot about the locked door, and I hurry downstairs to let him in.

He stares at me, a frown on his face. "What's gotten into you?"

"Sorry. I just felt nervous about being alone."

"Since when?" he asks, pushing past me and into the house. He empties his pockets on the counter and turns to me. "She looked good today, better than she has in a while."

I can see the evidence of this on his face. In his eyes. Instead of a serious, sad face, it's light and happy.

His words lift my spirits, and I put away thoughts of Mr. Elders. For now, anyway.

27

Light shines in Mom's room as I push through the door the next afternoon. Her large window is open, and a warm breeze stirs the air. It's the first time I've seen her room lit up like this.

She's propped up in bed, nibbling on broccoli.

"Mom, you look great!" My dad was right. She hasn't looked so good in three weeks.

She beams at me and takes another bite. "I feel good today. In fact..."

"Would you like to take a walk with us?" Fischer asks. He pushes through the door to Mom's room, rolling a chair with him. It's the first time I've ever seen a wheelchair, even though I've heard of them.

My gaze darts back to Mom. "You're going out?"

My mom smiles and nods. "That's right, the actual out-of-doors. Dr. Lane approved it when I told her how good I feel today."

My spirit feels as bright as the sunshine. This is progress. This is good. For the first time since her diagnosis, I allow myself to hope the nutritional diet will actually help Mom.

"Sure I'll come," I say. I lay my stuff in the chair, and then follow them into the hallway. We head toward the stairs. "Wait, how will you get the wheelchair outside?"

Fischer smiles. "Secret passage."

I frown, but when he pushes a button—the

elevator button—my heart speeds up. "We're riding the elevator?"

"We keep them running for emergencies like a fire. Dr. Lane approved it, so we can ride down. Your mom had to promise not to use the electrical lights in her room for a week."

"What? That sounds crazy."

My mom smiles and shakes her head. "No, it's not. It will be worth every moment."

We step inside the elevator and the doors slide shut. For a moment, I panic. What are we doing in the tiny box? What if we get stuck?

Fischer presses a button marked with a star, and the box jerks and starts moving. I count the dings, one, two. The box stops, and the doors open. The lobby sprawls out before me. I can't believe it.

Fischer wheels Mom out. "Aren't you coming?" he asks.

I snap my open mouth closed and step off. The doors slide shut behind me. I've done it. I've ridden an elevator. "That was great!"

My mom laughs, and we head outside.

The breeze feels like paradise, especially with Mom by my side. It lifts the hair from my neck, cooling me like ice on a steaming hot day.

"Look at those birds," Mom says. She points to a bird bath. "Can you roll me over there and let me watch?"

"Sure," Fischer says. "Do you like birds?"

My mom sighs. "I do now. I've learned to appreciate a lot of things since I've been cooped up for so long."

I know exactly what she means. I can't believe the things I miss—dinners together, evenings with nothing to do, even getting yelled at by Mom. I will never take the simple things for granted again.

A bird lands in the bath and flaps its wings, spraying an arc of water through the air. My mom laughs. The sound is like wedding bells ringing out in joy.

I watch her at first, but I get the feeling someone is looking at me. It's not the same feeling I've had for the past few days, this actually feels like someone is looking at me right this moment. I glance around and see Fischer staring at me. He smiles comfortably, but doesn't look away.

I do. Heat creeps up my neck.

I want to ask him about the honey-haired man and about God. Obviously now is not the time.

"How's Keegan?"

My mom's voice breaks through my musings. "Hmm?"

"Keegan. How is he? I haven't heard you talking about him lately."

Why is she asking this, and why right now? "I haven't really heard from him, actually. He's only written twice, but he sounds like he's having a good time and learning a lot."

"Good, I'm so glad. How are his parents?"

I haven't gone more than a day or two in my life without stopping to see Keegan's mom, Margaret, but I haven't talked to her since Mom got sick.

"I—I really don't know. They haven't come to visit, and I haven't had time to see them either. I've been here in my free time."

An understanding dawns in her eyes as she glances between Fischer and me. "Oh, of course. I hadn't thought of that."

Does Mom disapprove of an errant glance between me and Fischer? I can't believe she would. Maybe she just wants to know what's going on. She's from the military training center, after all. She likes to be in control. Do I get that from her, too?

The sun warms my arms and I take a deep breath. This is the first time I've been outside just for the sake of being outside in weeks. My mom living in the hospital is so hard; I'd forgotten all the normal joys in life. Things like hanging out with friends, and taking walks for no reason. Worrying about what to make for supper, instead of making it home from the hospital before curfew. The thought that I have ever lived a normal life is foreign to me.

"Do you remember when we used to go to the park when you were little?" Mom asks.

"Of course. Dad made a kite once." I can almost see the brown paper soaring in today's cloudless sky.

My mom smiles, staring into the past.

She's beautiful right here in this moment. Her cheeks are sunken, and her hair is limp and thin. She sits in a wheelchair, and her shoulders are slumped. It doesn't matter. Her eyes are alight, and she's beautiful.

All too soon, Fischer says, "I think we'd better head back in."

My mom nods and sighs. "I'm more tired than I care to admit."

I'm not ready for this wonderful outing to be over. We roll back to the elevator and step inside. Panic threatens me again, but it's definitely better the second time.

"I think I prefer the stairs," I say.

Fischer's eyebrows shoot up. "Really? I love the elevators."

"Do you ride them a lot?"

He chuckles. "No, this is only the third time. I still like them, though."

We step onto the third floor and wheel Mom back to her room. I help her into bed while Fischer takes the wheelchair out. "I'm so glad I came when I did," I say. "That was great."

My mom nods and smiles. "It was. I'm glad you came, too."

I move to sit down, but she puts her hand on my arm. "Hana, is everything OK with Keegan?" Her eyes have that worried look again.

"It's fine, Mom. You shouldn't be worried about him. I'm not." I'm surprised to realize I mean it.

My mom drifts off to sleep, and I relax into my chair.

After a while, Fischer brings me a glass of water. Again, I want to know more about him. "What do you really do on your day off?" I ask.

He smiles, his teeth like a fluffy white cloud. "I usually study."

I almost forget he's still in training. That makes me think of something else. "When do you go to class?"

"I don't have any classes, not exactly anyway. Most of my training is done in the hospital. This is my training."

"Do you ever relax, or go see your family or friends?" It seems like a stupid question, since I know he's not from my city. I know he's made at least some friends here, though. How else did he learn about God?

He shrugs. "Not too often. There's just not idle time in most of my days." He checks Mom's fluids and marks something on her chart before grinning at me.

"Why? Did you have something in mind?"

I will my cheeks not to turn red. "No." We couldn't get together and hang out if we wanted to. Single boys and girls don't hang out, and my "group" as it was is gone. I think of Ava, and wonder if she would like to do something with me.

He makes a few final checks and marks his clipboard. He's hanging around longer than usual. Finally, he speaks. "What did you think?"

At first, I'm confused, but then it hits me. He's talking about Mr. Elders. "I want to know more," I say. And I do. I'm not entirely sure I agree with the concept of God, but I'm willing to learn more.

The door pushes open, and Dr. Bentford steps into the room. "Hello, Hana. How are you?"

I smile on the outside, but inside I'm screaming. I want to have this conversation. Now. "I'm fine, Dr. Bentford. How are you?"

He smiles and begins checking Mom. "Good, thanks. We're going to have a special doctor in tomorrow. Will you be around to meet him?"

A special doctor? My heart soars. After her good day, this has to be a good sign. "I can't, I have school, and afterwards I have to use up our food allowances by the end of the week." Why didn't I buy food when I went to meet Mr. Elders? "What kind of specialist?" I ask.

"He sees patients around the country with the mutation. He develops personalized plans for them, to give them an optimal outcome. It's usually good to have family present to answer questions."

My spirits deflate. Maybe I don't have to use up our food allowance.

But I know that would be stupid. If we run out of

food next week, we won't get extra allowance. We'll have to starve until the next allowances are issued. Of course, we could always eat out of our garden.

Fischer slips out of the room, and I keep myself from sighing in frustration.

"She took a walk earlier today. That's a good sign, isn't it?"

"It certainly seems to be a step in the right direction."

The urge to plead her case overwhelms me, like this will be the last chance I get. "Isn't there anything more we can give her? Some type of real medication?"

He smiles at me like he's talking to a small child. "I'm sorry, Hana. It's not like the Early Days when they had access to all sorts of chemotherapy drugs. We have to work with what we've got." He makes a few final notations and nods at me. "Have a good day."

I can't believe he brought up chemo drugs. I want to throw my glass of water at him. Instead, I watch as he retreats from the room.

28

My mom doesn't wake up before curfew, so I kiss her forehead and slip from the room to head home. Ava steps out the front door of the hospital as I come from the stairs. I jog to catch up, and see her just as she puts something into her mouth—a pill, I presume.

"Hi, Ava."

Her eyes are red rimmed from crying. What could be bad enough to bring her down from her pill-high? "Oh, hi Hana. How's your mom?"

"She's the same, I guess. Any news on Markus?"

Ava shakes her head as we move outside. "They let my dad see him for a few minutes. Dad said he's hooked up to all kinds of machines. I didn't even know they had those kinds of machines. Anyway, we keep hoping they'll let someone else in, but they don't."

"Did you ever try to figure out what he was doing that night?" This is a dangerous question, I know. If Ava is in constant contact with the doctors for her pills then she could let something dangerous slip. Something like the fact I'm questioning her, or the fact that I'm suspicious about Markus in the first place.

"No, I wouldn't know where to start."

I don't tell her I've done my own investigation. We reach the corner where we split to go to our own blocks. I hate to leave her. "Ava, would you like to go to the market place with me?"

Her eyebrows shoot up, and her eyes light with—

pleasure? "Really? I'd love to!"

I wonder if she's as lonely as I am. "Great. What about tomorrow?"

"That would be great. I'll meet you after school?"

"Sure," I say.

She hesitates again. "So you have to give a speech on Saturday?"

Her question brings waves of nerves. I had forgotten about my speech—again. What am I going to say in front of all those people?

"I guess," I say. "I better get home and write one." I say it jokingly, like it's no big deal.

She laughs. "Right. I guess I'll see you later."

We wave and part ways. Even though we've never been friends before, we can understand each other. We both know how it feels to practically live at the hospital, and to walk in pain.

As I walk toward home, my mind goes back to graduation. My Test is ten days away. What if they send me away and Mom isn't better? The thought makes my stomach cramp up like it's being twisted in the washing machine.

Before I know where my feet are taking me, I'm at the levy. The sun hasn't disappeared completely, but it's sinking fast. In minutes I'll have to hurry home, but for now all I can do is stare across the river. I look toward the sky where the lights appeared two weeks ago. It seems like an eternity has passed.

Nothing's there tonight, and I run to make it home in time. I get to work making supper, but thoughts of Mom aren't far from my mind.

"Dad, did they say anything to you about a special doctor coming to see Mom tomorrow?" I ask over supper. We're sitting at the table, which is something we haven't done much of over the last few weeks.

"Sure. I'm pretty sure I'll be there. Why?"

"Dr. Bentford acted like I could come, too. I just wondered."

My dad smiles. "We're all encouraged by her progress. I'm sure the special doctor will have plenty to say. Don't worry about not being there. We'll get her fixed up."

I smile back, but my heart isn't in it. What if the doctor mentions chemotherapy as part of Mom's treatment? I know the chances are slim, but my hope just won't die.

What would the Greaters do to me if I skipped school just once?

Morning comes too quickly, and as I'm getting ready for school, there's a knock from the downstairs door. No one knocks on my door, ever. Even when Jamie used to come over, she generally just walked in.

My dad's already left for the agricultural center so I bolt downstairs and throw the door open. Fischer stands on the doorstep. "Morning."

My mouth drops open and I stare for what must be a full minute. Finally, my better sense takes over and I glance up and down the street to see if anyone's seeing this. The coast is clear. "What are you doing here?"

"You asked what I did on my days off. Today is a day off, and instead of spending it at the hospital like I usually do, I decided to relax. Per your suggestion."

I nod stupidly. "OK, but what are you doing here?"

He grins. "Would you like to spend the day with me?"

I truthfully don't understand what he's asking me.

We are single members of the opposite sex; we aren't allowed to spend the day together. Not only that, but I have school.

"You don't want to?" His smile falters ever so slightly, but his eyes still look hopeful. He reminds me of a stray dog begging for scraps. Just before a guard puts it down.

But still, his question flusters me. I tuck a stray strand of blond hair behind my ears. "I do, it's just that I can't. I have school, and I don't really want to make a habit of breaking laws." I'm surprised to realize I mean it. I *do* want to spend the day with him. A lot.

Guilt burns my insides like boiling water as I think of Keegan. He'll be home soon. What would he say about my feelings?

Still, how could Fischer suggest cutting school? No one cuts school, ever. Cutting even once can get you demoted, if the teachers deem it wasn't for a legitimate reason. Only slackers skip out on their duties, and slackers end up as Lessers.

My reasons don't faze him. He holds up a paper. "I have a pass."

I frown and take the paper, even though I know I need to hurry. I'm going to be late for school at this rate. I unfold it and read quickly. My head snaps up. "You have a medical pass?"

"It'll get you out of school for the day, so you can meet the specialist who's coming in to see your mom."

My heart swells up, and so do my eyes. I swipe in annoyance at the tears. A sudden urge to hug him in thanks sweeps over me, but I don't act on it. It doesn't matter if anyone is looking or not, that would be stupidly dangerous. "Thanks," I say instead, but then I frown. "I thought you said we would spend the day together. Away from the hospital."

"Meet me at noon, at the levies." He waves and continues down the street then, like being at my house first thing in the morning is the most natural thing in the world. He shoves his hands in his pockets and starts whistling some happy-sounding tune.

I glance down at the medical pass in my hand. I don't have to go to school today. I try to remember if I've ever missed an entire day of school, but I'm pretty sure the answer is no. I grab my bag and race to the hospital.

My mom sits up in bed when I come in the room, and Dad sits near her. "Hana!" she says. "What are you doing here?"

I slip into the other chair by her bed. "I got a medical pass. Dr. Bentford told me the specialist was coming today, and I really wanted to be here."

"I'm glad you're here, but I don't really see the significance of seeing a specialist. Honestly, what can they do any differently?" she says.

I want to tell her they can give her chemo drugs, but I keep that to myself. An hour passes, and then two. It's getting closer and closer to noon, and I don't want to miss my meeting with Fischer. So where is the specialist?

My mom drifts to sleep and I pick up one of her books.

"I wonder what's taking so long," Dad says. "I'm going to stretch my legs."

He steps from the room and I start my scan of the book. It's one that Jamie picked. I quickly put it down. I miss Jamie almost as much as I miss Mom being at home. We always walked home from school together. Sometimes, when our parents were in especially good moods, we even slept over at each other's houses.

That didn't happen too often just because our parents were always the tiniest bit afraid it was against the law—since technically we were out of our houses after curfew. Sometimes the guards did random sweeps of houses. They looked for contraband or laws being broken. I once heard of a family who had rigged the electrical meter to give them extra kilowatts. I guess they got demoted, too.

The door swings open and Dr. Bentford walks in. "Hana, you made it."

I spring out of my chair, anxious to hear what the new doctor is going to say. "Yeah, I got a medical pass. My dad's here, too. He went for a walk."

A second doctor enters the room. It's a large man—a really large man. I'm confused because I thought the Greaters had gotten rid of the obesity disease. I've never actually seen anyone who had it.

"This is Dr. Morgan. He'll be examining your mom."

Dr. Morgan sticks out his meaty hand, and I shake it eagerly. I don't even think about how strange it is for him to touch me, or how sweaty his hand is.

"It's nice to meet you," I say.

He gives me a slight smile, and we drop our hands. I notice his bald spot, and the way his upper lip beads with sweat. His nose is covered in enormous pores, and a few dark hairs curl out of it.

In spite of his gross appearance, I hope he can help Mom.

"What kind of treatments are you considering?" I blurt out. I know I should keep my mouth shut and let the doctor work, but I'm so nervous and on edge. Maybe he'll tell me he's come across a miracle food. Or a new medicine that's cheap to produce. Or a cure.

He doesn't do any of those things. "I'm afraid I don't have an answer for that yet. I'm just here to do a preliminary exam, and I'll come up with a plan of action after that." He doesn't even look at me while he speaks.

The doctor asks me questions about her previous habits: what foods did she normally eat, what exercises did she partake in, how many hours did she work. I can't see how any of that is relevant, but I answer patiently.

Then they awaken Mom so Dr. Morgan can ask her a few questions, too. My dad slips back into the room, and they introduce themselves.

After an hour the doctors leave. *That's it?* I want to scream at them. *Aren't you going to do something?* But I don't say any of that, because doctors are Greaters, and we're not permitted to question the Greaters.

I glance at the clock on the wall. Five till noon. I sigh. At least I'll meet Fischer on time.

29

The sun warms my arms as I walk down the broken sidewalks. I'm glad it's almost summer time. I like the warm better than the cold, especially since I'm already shivering. Breaking the law isn't one of the most natural things in the world for me.

What will Fischer talk about? God? I can't deny I'd be interested to learn more.

I don't take the path directly from my house. Instead, I go past Ava's house and take the beaten path from there. I don't know which path Fischer took, but I doubt he knows where Ava lives, and it's doubtful he used this one. I don't want anyone to think we're meeting each other.

I see him long before he sees me. He faces the river, leaning back on his elbows, staring up at the sky. His brown hair glows in the light.

For the first time since meeting him, I let myself think he's attractive. Not that I haven't felt it before, I just haven't let myself think about it. I always push the thought away, and replace it with something about Mom, or Keegan, or Jamie. Or even Ava and Markus.

"Hey," I say lightly.

He spins around, and I give a little wave.

"How did it go with the specialist?" he asks.

"It could have been better, I think."

He pats the green grass beside him and I sit cross legged. "The doctor said he was just there to do a preliminary exam. He said he would work a plan up from there."

Fischer watches me speak, not interrupting or pushing his thoughts on me. I'm glad for this. He's a good listener. When I'm done talking, he turns back to the river and resumes his leaning position.

How can he be so relaxed? I can't stop glancing around like the guards are just waiting for me to let my guard down.

"I only have six months left of my training," he says casually.

This surprises me, though it really shouldn't. I try to think of what he wants me to say. "What will you do then? Are you planning to go back to your own city?"

He shakes his head. "I doubt they'll assign me there."

This is a strange answer. "Why not?" In fact, it would be unusual for them to *not* assign him to his home city.

"Look at that bird," he says instead of answering me. He points to a huge black raven circling something dead on the bank across the river. "It can go wherever it wants to go. It doesn't have to worry about food allowance, or medical allowance, or electrical allowance."

He's going somewhere with this, but I can't think of where. I like listening to him talk, though. His voice is like music, his words a song.

This is why he makes a great medic, I realize. Whenever he speaks he calms people. Makes them feel better. Helps them rationalize instead of freak out over the scary medical things they're facing.

"It can return to its family if it chooses. No one keeps them apart."

I immediately remember his strange behavior on the hospital roof a few days ago. I had said it was hard being separated from your family, and he'd cringed ever so slightly. This is why he was against the Greaters and their system. I'm sure of it.

"Who's keeping you from your family?" I ask softly.

He takes his time turning to me. It's not because he's trying to ignore me, or to show me he'll speak when he's ready. It's because of the pain I see in his eyes. He doesn't want me to see it.

My heart warms to him, and I want to do something—anything—to comfort him.

"*They* are," he says.

The Greaters. I don't know why I asked, other than I wanted to hear him admit it. Fischer is so perfect, like an arching rainbow in the sky after a rainstorm. I want to be sure he's human, that he has cracks like me.

"Where are they?" I ask.

He takes a deep breath and turns back to the levy. "I would go back there in a heartbeat, if they'd assign me to the hospital there. They don't send Lessers back to their home cities, though."

I freeze. I definitely hadn't expected this. At all.

"You were a *Lesser*?" the words come out much harsher than I'd intended, but he doesn't seem to notice.

He nods. "I took my Test and scored as a Middle. I was shipped out the next day. I didn't even get to say goodbye to my family."

A million questions run through my head. Was his life horrible growing up? Had he starved or lived without electricity? Had he lived in squalor?

But then I remember his words—he would go

back in a heartbeat.

"It's not like they told you," he says, as if he can read my mind. "My Lesser city, I mean. The people aren't scum. They're not all drug addicts, even though they would be if the Greaters had their way. They're not all criminals. We're just people. My parents taught me about God."

God.

If God is a Lesser concept, how can I really put any stock in it? I hear what he's saying about their cities, how they're not all bad. But I've seen pictures of the filth, of the sickly and unattractive people. I can't reconcile the two images.

Fischer has to be an exception.

"My friend Jamie was just demoted." It's out before I can stop it. I haven't talked to anyone about it, not even Dad.

He turns to look at me now. "What for?" No condemnation, just curiosity and understanding.

"She got pregnant and refused an abortion."

"I'm sorry. You must miss her."

"I do," I squeak out. "Will she be OK?" For the first time I feel relief. Here is someone who might know what Jamie's life will be like.

"If she's anything like you, she'll be fine." His eyes bore into mine, and I swallow the lump in my throat.

I'm not sure how to take that, but I guess it's a good thing. "Were you born Lesser?" I ask.

"Yep. My parents were demoted before I was born because they believed in God. They refused to meditate just because they refused to follow the Greaters' form of teachings."

Icy fear trickles down my neck, intermingled with sweat. How did the Greaters know his parents weren't meditating? I haven't meditated in at least a week. I picture my own room and determine to keep my curtains pulled shut from now on.

"They were demoted to keep them quiet, but when it didn't work they were threatened."

I frown. "With what?"

He looks at me, his eyes wide. "Execution." Like I should know this already. "My mom had just found out she was expecting me, and they knew it wouldn't do anyone any good for them to be dead. So they went underground."

Underground. I know he doesn't mean it literally, as in they didn't actually dig a hole. But I'm not sure exactly what it does mean, either.

"I don't understand about God," I say. "How does anyone know anything about Him? How did your parents know about Him?"

He sits up now, his face lit with excitement. "There's a book."

This seems too simple. "I've read dozens of books recovered from digs. I've never read one that mentioned God, at least not in a serious way."

He laughs. "Or course not. They burn the books that deal with religion, or politics, or freedom."

I remember that day in Mrs. Baily's bookstore, and how she reacted when I saw a book she hadn't removed in time. I know he's telling the truth.

"The Holy Bible," I say.

"That's right."

"But how have you seen a Bible? Do Lessers have them?"

"Not most, but those in the underground have them. My parents had one, and Mr. Elders has one. I've read it."

I glance around once again. I'm not as nervous now about being caught with Fischer as I am about being caught taking part in this conversation. Still, it's too unreal to not make me curious. A forbidden book that tells me about a real God? People in my own city who are spreading His message?

I want to know more. "How can I see it?"

He watches me, gauging my sincerity. "Why do you want to learn about this? Just to rebel against the Greaters, or because you really want to know God?"

"Does it matter?" I ask.

He watches me again, and then he shrugs. "I'll do what I can."

We don't talk about the Bible anymore. I glance around again, and when I'm sure no one is watching us I lay down in the soft grass beside him. It's cool and soft, like a pillow. A second bird joins the first in a swirling dance across the sky.

My arm is only centimeters from Fischer's, and I can almost feel the sparks between our skin.

"Tell me about your city," I say. "Tell me about how you grew up."

He lies beside me, watching the birds too. "My mom kept the house spotless. I promise you've never seen such a clean house. It was impossible to play like a normal kid." He laughs as he says this.

I stop watching the birds to watch him. His cheeks are round and rosy with his happy remembering. I'm fascinated by him. "We prayed before every meal."

I don't stop him but I have no idea what pray means.

"My dad played with me every night when he got home from work."

His description of life doesn't match up with what

we've been taught in school. At all. His life sounds happy, clean, and normal. "Where does your dad work?"

Fischer turns to me now. "He's a janitor at the Lesser hospital in our city. I used to visit him. That's where I figured out I wanted to be a medic."

His story is unusual, I think. We were taught the Lessers rarely took their Test, and even if they did they didn't make it past Lesser.

I pick a blade of grass and rub it between my fingers. "Do you have any brothers or sisters?"

"No. You're allowed two children here in the Middle cities, but in the Lesser cities you're only allowed one."

My eyes widen. "Really?" I prop myself up on my elbows. "What about your allowances? Do Lessers get different allowances?"

His eyes lose focus, like he's searching the air behind me. "We got the same food allowance, but less electrical allowance and medical allowance."

We get such a meager electrical allowance here. How can anyone survive on less, especially in the winter?

"The worst part is that the Lessers can trade any of their allowances for extra entertainment allowance."

This is hard to believe. We're not allowed to trade allowances, period. If you're caught, you can be punished. "Why would they want the Lessers to spend more on entertainment?"

Again he looks at me as if I should have this figured out. "Entertainment is where the Greaters make the most money. If the Greaters have to spend less on food for the people, that's just money in their pockets." He doesn't stop there, though. "If you have any medical problems they don't treat them. They put you on the pills. Once you're hooked, they know you won't be any trouble."

An invisible hand clenches around my stomach. "Is that what they're doing to Ava?"

He watches me innocently for what seems like ever. Finally, he shakes his head and shrugs. "I don't know, Hana. They may be trying to get her through the tough time with her brother and nothing more. Her father was a Greater, wasn't he?"

I nod.

"Then I doubt they'd try and get her hooked on anything."

That doesn't really reassure me.

"Why'd you meet me here today?" Fischer asks. He's propped up on one elbow now, facing me.

"You asked me to," I remind him. But I have a feeling he's asking for a deeper answer. I'm not sure I can give him one, even though I want to ask him why he asked me here himself.

He smiles. "I'm glad you came. I haven't spent much time socializing since I've come, except for meetings with the underground."

"You've been here for your whole training?" I ask.

He nods and lies back down.

So he was here before Mom got the mutation. He was here before Jamie even met Easton. He was here before Keegan took his Test and left the city. He was here, in that hospital, for the past few years, and I never knew it.

"I wish I had met you back then," I say. I immediately regret it, but the smile he gives me melts my heart, and I change my mind. I'm glad I told him. I like being the one to make him smile.

"Tell me about how you grew up," he says now. "In all the gory detail."

I laugh loudly. "Nothing gory about it, only boring. I played outside with Jamie and Keegan, both my neighbors. Both of my parents work at the local colleges, and they have my whole life. There was no—praying—before we ate, and no talk about God. We did meditate though. A lot."

"Jamie's your best friend you mentioned earlier?"

My throat feels small again. I swallow and nod.

"And Keegan?"

Do I imagine the suddenly serious tone behind his words? I hesitate only a fraction of a second before answering. "He's my other best friend, or he was before he tested and left for his training." I push away the guilt of not admitting he's more than a friend.

"What's his profession?"

"He's in entertainment," I say. How would Keegan feel about padding the Greaters' pockets? What does Fischer think of this?

"You Test soon." It's a statement, and he says it while staring at the sky.

"Yes," I say. "In a few days." I'm beginning to wonder if there's something wrong with my throat. Why's it so swollen today? It can't be the tears I keep trying to fight back.

He looks at me now. "You're going to do great, and you're going to get the profession you want."

But he doesn't state the obvious, that I'll be sent away to train in another city. Away from him, and away from Mom. I don't bring it up either.

We lie in silence for a while. It feels nice just to be together for no reason. I haven't done that in a long time.

"You're going to the market?" he asks.

I had almost forgotten. "Yes, after school. I'm meeting Ava. I guess I should go."

He sits up, raking his hand through his hair to dislodge grass and dirt. "Go to the park tomorrow after school. Mr. Elders will meet you then."

His words come out of nowhere, and I'm surprised. "What for?"

"You said you wanted to know more about the Bible. I'll make sure you get to."

I'm not even sure how to thank him. I stare at him for way too long, my heart beating faster with every second. He stares right back until finally I look away.

We both stand up and brush off our pants.

"I'm glad you talked me into taking a day off," he says, grinning.

I smile too, sad that it's over. "I'll see you around?"

"Right. See you."

We take separate routes home.

30

I get to the school just as the first students trickle out the front doors.

Ava peers through the crowd, her eyes scanning the other kids, her face laced with confusion.

I wave my arm above my head to get her attention. She sees me just as she pops something in her mouth. I cringe. How many of those things does she take a day? The doctors must have given her an unlimited supply.

She meets me on the sidewalk. "Where have you been all day?" she asks. "I didn't see you in any of our classes."

I wish she was Jamie, and then I could tell her about Fischer. Instead, I shrug. "I got a medical pass because of Mom. She had a special doctor evaluating her today." We start toward the market place.

"Aren't we going to meditate first?" Ava asks. "I thought you always did that after school."

I think of Fischer's parents, and I fleetingly wonder why they don't just give us all pills, but then I realize that would be too expensive. Should I say I meditate at night? I don't want to lie. "We can if you want to."

She shakes her head. "No, I don't really do that anymore either."

I don't ask why because the reason is pretty obvious.

The weather is warm and friendly and nice. It shows in the citizens of our city because people mingle on the sidewalks and in the streets, instead of staying holed up in their cold houses wrapped in coats and blankets. The clatter of voices permeates the air. It's a warm feeling, a welcome feeling. The camaraderie of the people feels safe.

"Did you bring any allowances with you?" I ask.

She shakes her head like it's no big deal, but her eyes look clouded. I realize she's hiding something. Maybe they already used their allowances for the week, but why would she need to hide that?

"I'm glad you could come with me. I get lonely without Mom around," I say.

"Or your other friend, too, I bet."

My breath catches, but I force myself on. This is the first time someone's mentioned Jamie to me, but of course Ava would have noticed. "Yeah, that too," I say.

We walk a few moments in silence. "I saw you taking another pill," I say casually. "They must really be helping."

"They are. I feel so much better with them. Even Mom has started taking them."

"So Markus isn't doing any better?"

"No, not really."

We fall silent again. I want to know what she's keeping from me, so I say, "I don't mind swinging by your house, if you want to get your allowance vouchers."

She shakes her head. "No, I think we're OK on food."

I don't believe her for a second, but it's apparent she's not giving up her secret yet.

The market place is busy today. Food allowances

are issued on varying days each week, this way everyone staggers their visits. But I guess everyone wants to enjoy the sunshine today.

"I haven't been to the market lately," Ava says. "Is it always this busy?"

I look at her. Her black hair glimmers in the sun, and I realize it's greasy. The more I study her the more I see other upsetting things. Her arms are too skinny, and her cheeks look hollow. I wonder when she ate last.

"Not always," I say, and I pull her toward the fruit table and buy two pears. "Here." I shove one into her hands. "Eat with me. I feel weird eating alone." It's a lie, but I don't feel guilty for saying it. And technically, we just broke the law, since sharing allowances isn't allowed, but Ava needs to eat. Whatever is in those pills she takes isn't good for her.

Again Fischer's stories come back to me. Something nags at the back of my brain, but I can't put my finger on it.

We fight our way through the throngs to browse what's available. The merchandise changes from time to time, depending on growing seasons.

We come to a vegetable table and I see fat ears of corn. The color is good, and I bet even Dad would appreciate how well this produce turned out. I decide to buy two ears for supper that night, just to show him, but when I look up at the seller I freeze.

Easton stands with his dad at their produce table. He looks pale, and I think there's even a faint bruise on one cheek, but he's here.

Easton has not been transferred to a Lesser city.

Easton abandoned Jamie.

Burning hot steam rises in my belly. It works its

way up to my chest, and then my whole head feels like it's in an oven. I'm on fire. The heat consumes me. It melts me.

I want to scream. I want to hit him.

I want to cry. Poor Jamie. My dear, sweet Jamie all alone in a Lesser city. At least I assume that's where she is, since she swore she wouldn't abort her baby.

Their baby.

"How much for the corn?" I demand. I'm not even trying to be civil, and I really just want him to notice me.

He glances at me now, noting my voice dripping with hatred. He sees me and freezes. At first he says nothing, but finally he squeaks out, "Two allowances."

I stuff the ears in my bag but don't give him my allowance voucher. "You can put those on Jamie's bill," I say and walk away.

A few people stare at me, their eyes wide with surprise. I can practically hear their thoughts...*Did that girl just steal corn from the produce table?*

I don't care what they think.

I storm through the crowd, Ava hot on my heels. I feel a little guilty when I remember Ava. The poor thing is probably having a panic attack right about now. Almost on cue, she pops another tiny pill.

Something grabs my arm like a metal clamp. Strong fingers dig into my flesh and spin me around.

I'm staring into Easton's anxious face.

For a moment I'm frozen, as still as stone. I can't believe he's touching me. Sure, most people don't touch—but for a boy to touch a girl isn't just strange. It's illegal.

"Let go," I demand.

He does, immediately. A few people still watch us

curiously. Anxiously.

I have the good sense to glance around for guards, but I think I'm safe for the moment.

"Can you tell me what's going on?" His voice cracks on the last word and I don't understand why. It's almost like he's going to cry.

"What are you talking about?" I ask. He must know what's going on. His table was absent the other day, right after they took Jamie. And he's got faded bruises to prove he was in some sort of altercation.

"Where did they take Jamie?" he says. "After the procedure, I mean? They said she would come home after the procedure."

The world suddenly swirls around me, like a toy top I used to play with as a little kid. It's so fast I'm afraid I might throw up.

I must look pretty bad because Ava takes my wrist softly in her hands. "Are you OK?" she asks.

"What are you talking about?" I say. "What procedure?"

Easton swallows hard and shifts from foot to foot. "You know," he says, glancing around. "After they aborted the pregnancy."

"What's going on here?" someone asks. It's Easton's father. He looks seriously unhappy with his forehead wrinkled up and his mouth drooping down.

"She's a friend from school," Easton says. "It's fine."

"I'm no friend of yours," I say, just as his dad says, "Well, I need you back at the table. Move it."

We all stare at each other for one long, uncomfortable moment.

"I'll be right there, Dad," Easton says.

His dad gives him a scathing look but fights his

way back to their table.

"She didn't have the procedure," I say. "She swore she wasn't going to. It wasn't what she wanted." I know my words are true. Jamie wouldn't have given in, would she?

Easton glances nervously at his dad. "There's too much to explain, and I don't know what's going on myself. We need to meet somewhere. Will you meet me?"

I can't believe he's asking me this. Doesn't he realize how much trouble he's already caused by asking girls to meet him?

Still, the need to know how Jamie was after they took her wins out. "Where?"

"Tonight," he says. "I'll knock on your door three times."

I don't ask what time. I don't need to know, because I'll be awake regardless.

"Fine," I say. "I'll be waiting."

31

Ava's oddly calm as we leave the market place. I feel people's gaze on us as we walk, and I finally have the good sense to care. What if they turn us in? Someone there is bound to know at least one of us.

"You didn't get any food," Ava says.

"I don't care." Which is true, but Dad will care when we don't have any food to eat for supper. Which means I'm going to have to go back. I sigh. "Can we just hang out at your house for a little while? Until the crowd at the market changes?"

She nods. "Of course." We walk there quickly, eager to get out of the open.

Her house looks eerily abandoned. Dust covers the table, the chairs, and their radio. Dirty dishes are piled in the sink. The dried food on the plates is discolored and hard, and I can tell the dishes have been there a while.

"I have to go to the bathroom," Ava says. She slips into the hallway and I hear a door close.

The drapes are all pulled and the house is dark. I flip a light switch but nothing happens. I frown. That's odd, but maybe they've used all their electrical allowance for the month.

My mouth is hot and dry from all the excitement with Easton, so I open a cabinet to grab a glass, but the cabinet is empty. I open another, and another, and another. They're all empty.

Finally, I find a single cabinet with a few dishes. I grab a glass and turn on the water. Only a trickle comes out.

Ava comes up behind me. "What do you need?"

"I was thirsty," I say. Something is very wrong with this picture.

She smiles. "Yeah, our water is kind of pathetic. We don't get very much, so you have to hold your glass under there for a while to fill it up."

I shake my head and set the glass down. "Ava, you should have enough water allowance for your own family. If this is all you have there is something wrong."

She shrugs and sits on a stool at her counter. "There's nothing wrong, Hana. Trust me."

"Ava, why don't you have any food or electricity?"

Her eyes widen and her mouth drops open a fraction. She seems surprised I noticed. "Sometimes the Greaters let you trade one allowance for another, when you need it."

That nagging I felt earlier comes back full force. I hear what she says, but I can hardly believe it. "You traded all of your allowances? For what?"

She looks at the counter and traces her finger in the dust. "Medical allowance," she says in a small voice.

"For Markus?" I doubt this, but I want to make sure. After all, what would they be doing to him that would require such high medical allowance? They wouldn't let the family give up food, electricity, and water to pay for it. They would simply move Markus to a Lesser hospital.

She shakes her head, confirming my suspicion.

"Not for him. For us."

It dawns on me then and I get that throw up feeling in my throat. "To pay for your pills."

She nods.

I grab her shoulders as gently as I can and shake her. "Ava, you have to stop taking them. Don't you see what's happening?"

"I can't help it, Hana. I need them."

"No, you need food, Ava! And water! You can't live without those things."

She shrugs. She still won't look at me.

I can't believe the Greaters would let this happen. Whatever Markus was doing that night was big. Otherwise, the Greaters wouldn't be going to such lengths to keep the family quiet.

We're all in their hands, I realize. We're their puppets, keeping their country running so they can continue to rule unquestioned. I don't feel sick at the thought, but I do feel determined. I am determined to stop them.

"Ava, promise me you won't do it this month. You have to eat. You have to drink! You'll die."

She pulls away from me limply. "OK, I won't trade this month. I'll only get the pills I can buy with my regular medical allowance."

I search her eyes for deception, but they're so hollow I can't tell a thing. I have to take her word for it.

When enough time passes, I get ready to leave. "Are you sure you don't want me to come?" Ava asks.

"That's OK," I say. "There's no need for both of us to humiliate ourselves further."

Ava smiles and gives me a hug. I wonder why we've gone all this time without touching other people in our society. It really is growing on me. "I'll see you around," she says.

I leave Ava at her house and head back to the market. Easton and his dad are gone, thankfully. The other vendors haven't forgotten my outburst, though, and they watch me warily. I buy eggs, remembering a few weeks ago when I came with Jamie and she bought some. I get a few other necessary items and hurry home. Easton's words replay in my mind, and I worry for Jamie. Did they make her have an abortion?

I turn the corner onto my street just as I realize I made a mistake. A big, glaring mistake. I agreed to meet Easton right in front of Ava. Kindhearted, loveable, unstable Ava. Will she tell anyone? What if she wants her pills and they won't give them to her? Will she give me up?

I can't believe I was so stupid.

I slip inside my house and lock the door—it's obviously becoming a habit.

Big blunder or not, tonight can't come fast enough.

32

The moon is high overhead, but I'm not at all tired. I pace my small room. Back and forth, back and forth. I don't dare look out my window in case a passing guard glances up. My dad's been asleep for at least two hours. How long is Easton going to make me wait?

Somewhere an owl hoots. A stray dog barks. A knock echoes.

Sprinting downstairs, I wipe my sweaty hands on my bed pants. Easton slips inside as soon as I open the back door.

"Is it safe?" he asks.

"Yes, my dad's been asleep for hours." I have no idea if he's a light sleeper, though. I've never tested him to find out. "Tell me what happened." I can't wait another moment to hear how Jamie was. My heart aches at the thought of her pain, and I miss her.

His hands shake, and so does his voice. "They locked me in a room and asked me a bunch of questions. They wanted to know how we'd met, where we snuck around, and who helped us. I kept telling them *no one* helped us, but they didn't believe me. They kept saying things about our group, and I just kept telling them there wasn't a group."

A group? They think Jamie and Easton are part of the rebellion. "What did you say?"

"I told them the truth. We'd met at school and just snuck around here and there when Jamie didn't have anything to do, or when we didn't have class."

"How was Jamie?"

He shakes his head. "They wouldn't tell me about her at first. They kept saying she was having her procedure. Finally, they said she'd come back home as soon as the procedure was finished. I've been waiting to see her, but I haven't yet."

Anger and irritation bubble up my spine. "You mean you never actually saw her?"

He shakes his head.

I work to keep my voice low. All this and I'm not going to find out how she was. "What do you mean you never saw her? How do you know they were telling the truth? How do you know they didn't send her away to some Lesser city while you go on with your life?"

He wipes at his eyes, his chin quivering. "I wanted to go with her. I promised her I would. They told me she chose to have the procedure. They said she'd agreed to never see me again."

"Jamie wouldn't have done that," I say. And I'm sure of it. Jamie wanted to be with Easton more than anything, and she wouldn't have chosen to have the procedure and stay away from him.

A thought hits me. "They lied to her."

"What?"

"They told her you didn't want her. They said you'd chosen to stay here without her, and then they sent her away."

Realization lights his eyes and they fill with fresh tears. "I didn't say that!" His words are too loud.

"Shh!" I hiss, glancing at the stairs. "I said they lied, didn't I?" I don't have much patience for him. "I still don't think she had the procedure. I think they sent her away." It makes perfect sense to me. Easton is a promising agriculturist. They don't like losing productive members of society.

He crumples to the floor, covering his eyes with his hands. "I'll never see her again."

He's probably right, but I don't say so. "I'll see what I can find out. I'll be in touch if I find anything."

He glances up from his seat in the floor. "Why are you helping me?"

"I'm not helping you. I'm helping Jamie." And it's true. I don't really care about Easton or his problems. In fact, I think I blame him for all this.

A spark of guilt nags at me. I glance at him, sitting like a wounded animal in my kitchen floor. Maybe I do pity him, just a little.

A floor board creaks above our heads. I yank on his arms and pull him to his feet. "Get out of here before my dad catches you."

A soft thump, thump, thump sounds. "He's coming. Go!"

Easton moves like thick sludge, shuffling toward the door. My dad's at the bottom of the stairs, and I quickly shut the door behind Easton and grab a glass from the counter.

"Hana? What are you doing down here in the middle of the night?"

I pretend to drink. "I was thirsty."

"I thought I heard voices."

"Hmm, maybe it was a dog. I keep hearing some mutt barking up a storm. It's why I can't sleep."

He watches me like he's weighing my words, but just then a dog starts howling down the street.

I roll my eyes. "Dumb mutt."

I can tell he's not buying it all the way. "Don't

forget what we've talked about, Hana."

"I won't, Dad." I congratulate myself on keeping my voice steady and will my heart rate to slow. I feel like I should tell him the truth. I hate lying to him, but judging by his previous reactions to what's been going on, I don't think he'd be very understanding.

He stares for one last moment. "Hurry to bed, Hana."

"Goodnight, Dad. I'm on my way up."

He disappears up the stairs after one last scathing look, and I let out a rushing breath. I hurry to the window and peek out just as a shadow passes the window. It seemed awfully short for Easton, but at least he got away.

33

We have six days left of school. How has it passed in such a blur? I still don't have a speech, but when we practice our graduation march and ceremony, I pretend I'm perfectly prepared. I just want to get through the day so I can meet Mr. Elders at the park.

"How's your mom doing?" Mrs. Sewell asks.

"She was doing well yesterday. She saw a special doctor who's supposed to set up a better treatment plan for her."

Mrs. Sewell's eyes widen. "That's great, Hana! I'm so glad to hear it. I want your mind to be at ease with the Test coming up. You've seemed so beaten down lately."

Have I? If she's noticed, then I've been taking too many chances, drawing too much attention.

"I'll be ready," I assure her.

"I'm sure of it." She smiles and moves on.

Finally, the day ends and school is out. I hurry out of the building, not bothering to look around for Ava or anyone else.

I head straight toward the park, but something catches my eye. It's Lilith, standing beside a tree watching me walk. Again, she doesn't look hateful, just curious. She doesn't even turn away when I catch her looking.

I keep walking and try to ignore her.

The weather is just as warm as yesterday, and I

peel my sweater off and wrap it around my waist.

Nerves jump in my stomach. I don't like meeting Mr. Elders like this, out in the open. I don't have a reason to be at the park, and I'm afraid I'll be stopped. My dad's warnings ring in my ears. He made his threat before Jamie was turned in. After seeing her be dragged away, would he really be willing to put me through the same thing? Wasn't there any love for his own daughter? Since when do parents turn over their own offspring?

I get to the park, and it turns out I don't have to worry about standing out. There's some kind of celebration going on. A party. People crowd the beautiful green grass throughout Forest Park.

I wander through the people, getting bumped and elbowed. I didn't even know there were this many people in the city. There are so few of us, and the city is so large, it's easy to lose sight of how many of us there really are. The people smile, laugh, talk loudly. It feels safe. I feel hidden.

Someone bumps into me and I mutter, "Excuse me."

Something sharp pokes my hand, and I frown. I realize the honey-haired man is moving away from me. I look down at my hand and see a folded piece of paper. Our meeting must be over. Disappointment washes over me. I had hoped to speak with him at length again. I have so many questions, and no time to get answers.

I shove the paper in my pocket and go to the hospital.

Fischer talks with Dr. Bentford in the hallway. We all smile at each other as I pass, and I go straight to Mom's room.

"Hi, Mom."

Her eyes are yellowed, and her lips are cracking and dry. I'm shocked by how bad she looks. How did it happen so fast?

"Hana, I've missed you." She's making herself be cheerful, I can tell.

I glance at her bag of fluids. It drip, drip, drips into the IV line attached to her arm.

"How are you, Mom?"

She smiles and shrugs. It comes out more as a grimace. "You know. Same as always."

How could she feel so good one day, and so bad a couple days later? "Are you eating?"

She hates it when I ask this question, which I do, every day. It's the only chance she has at getting better. She has to eat the fruits and vegetables, or she has no shot.

"You know it's the only hope we have," I say.

"I know, Hana. I eat a little each day. That's all I can manage."

I don't push the issue. The note in my pocket puts me on edge, and I can't read it until I'm alone. I don't want to take my frustrations out on Mom.

I take a deep breath to calm my nerves, and I sit beside the bed. "Did you finish the other book?" One of the books I bought her lays on the bedside table.

"Yes, it was really good. Jamie picked that one didn't she?"

Jamie's name stings a little, but I nod. "How did you know?"

Mom smiles for real this time. "You girls are so different and yet so the same. I could tell she would pick something like that. Will you tell her I knew?"

Her words bring relief to my heart. What did

Fischer say yesterday? If Jamie's anything like me, she'll be fine. So maybe she will. "The next time I see her, I promise." I don't tell her that I probably won't see Jamie again. That Jamie is most likely far away from us and will be for the rest of her life.

I've always been able to talk to Mom about anything. Everything. I want to tell her about Jamie and Ava, and even about Fischer and my confusing feelings for him. I want to ask her about God, but I'm too afraid. What if she mentions it to someone else, even offhandedly? It's too dangerous. Fischer's family is proof.

"You look upset," Mom says. "I mean, more than usual."

She knows me so well. I toy with the idea of telling her the truth. I stare at my hands for long moments before meeting her eyes. "I've been thinking about some things, Mom."

"What kind of things?"

Where to start? I can't deny I admire Fischer, a lot. The fact that he believes in this God goes a long way. I want to believe him. I want to trust him, and I want to look for God myself. And maybe, if there is a God, He can save Mom.

"I know religion is against the law," I say softly. The door to the room is closed, so I know no one in the hall can hear me, but still I worry. Her face doesn't register shock or anger, so I go on. "But I've heard some talk lately. Talk about God."

My mom watches my face for a second, and then sighs and looks at the ceiling. "I'm not surprised, Hana. You and Jamie are alike, but you and I are alike too."

It takes a moment for what she's saying to kick in.

I gasp. "You've been thinking about this too?"

She smiles a little guiltily. "I think it must be natural when you're faced with death, but I've always wondered about God. There were things I heard years ago. They've stuck with me, but I never sought out answers. I was too afraid."

"Mom, don't talk about death," I say.

But Mom holds up her hand. "Don't argue about it, Hana. We all know what the mutation does. I'm just saying, I've been wondering what happens after I die."

"You'll come back," I say automatically. I hope she's going to refute this.

"I know, I know. But is that true? I'm not sure I believe it. Not entirely."

I take a shaky breath. I can't bear to think of Mom's death, and a dull ache starts behind my eyes. "So what happens if we don't come back?"

She keeps her eyes on the ceiling. "I don't know, Hana. I wish I did."

Something hardens in me, in my mind. I make a resolution. If there is another answer to be found then I will find it. My mom deserves to know. My mom needs to know. She seems reserved to her death. I am far from reserved. I not only want to find answers for her, I want to find a cure for her. There is only one thing I know of to help her—chemo drugs. I don't care if I have to die for them, I will get them for her, but more than that I'm going to find out what happens if she does die.

"Where did you hear about God, Hana?"

I shrug, unwilling to tell her the truth. If she were to accidently let the information slip, I don't want anyone else getting in trouble. "Just around. People talk all the time."

She seems to believe me, but what's more, she seems to believe in God. I feel the wall around my heart crumbling just a little.

I don't stay at the hospital much longer. The note from Mr. Elders calls my attention. Fischer isn't in the hall when I leave. It's the first time I've come to see Mom that I haven't spoken with him. I almost miss him.

Guilt plays with my mind, but I push it aside. Keegan is far away and so is Jamie now. I'm allowed a friend, aren't I?

Ava's face pops into my head. Maybe I should go see her. I 'm worried about her, and I want to make sure there's nothing dangerous between us. Does she remember I agreed to meet Easton? Has she told anyone? I definitely need to see her. Maybe I can talk her out of taking the pills. I finish my walk home with the determination to track her down at school.

34

My dad isn't home when I get there. I hurry to my room and shut the door behind me, and my eyes immediately look to Jamie's window across the alley. It's a habit I'll have to break. For now, I just close the curtains.

I flip off my shoes and sit cross-legged on my bed. Mr. Elders's note is two pages long.

The Holy Bible is God's book. It was penned by men over 2100 years ago, by inspiration of God. We can know that His words are sure and right, because He promises us they are. Ever since the words were first written there have been evil men who have tried to obliterate them.

One hundred years ago, evil men almost succeeded.

After the great disasters of the Early Days, most of man's knowledge and access to technology was lost. The survivors of the disasters banned together and started the cities we now know. They formed laws to keep the cities moving smoothly and safely. Laws that would keep the people fed and cared for. Some of these laws were questionable, but everyone agreed they were for the best. We believe that t*he head of those people, the first Greaters, realized that if man followed the Bible, they wouldn't always agree with the Greaters' new laws. So the Greaters outlawed religion. It was an easy sell—the wars throughout time have all been religious wars. The people had moved away from God and cared nothing for religion anymore. They were tired of the morals, hardships, and fighting, and they just wanted* *peace.*

They willingly gave up God.

There were a few who disagreed, and they went into hiding. They worked to find Bibles and other holy scripts. These artifacts are kept closely guarded.

Over the years, generations have completely forgotten about God. Your generation doesn't know Him or His laws at all. You've never heard of heaven or hell or right versus wrong. You only know what the Greaters have told you, which isn't much. Lawlessness is allowed and even encouraged in Lesser cities. Their excess works to the Greaters' profit.

Middle cities are kept running smoothly, because if it weren't for the Middles, the Greaters would have to do the heavy lifting themselves.

The Greaters have access to more information than you can imagine. They even have religion themselves—only not the true religion. They have deceived themselves, and they worship various gods. Gods that neither see nor hear. But they would never admit this. It would cause rioting and uproar among the people.

It is the same with the chemo drugs, and why they are kept secret. The best things are reserved for the better people. At least those who are better in the Greaters' eyes.

Change is coming. There are more who are ready than you know.

I stare at those last words and try to process them. There are more than I know? Who? Fischer of course. Who else? Have they read the Bible?

More than ever I want my hands on this book. I will beg and plead with Fischer if I have to. I don't want the answers only for myself anymore. I need them for Mom, and for Jamie locked away behind Lesser gates.

I scan the part of the letter that says lawlessness is allowed and encouraged in the Lesser cities. Fischer hinted at this when he said the Lessers are given pills and are encouraged to trade their allowances for entertainment. Of course, I know that there is more crime there. The people are violent, which is why most aren't allowed into the Middle cities.

I try to reconcile this with what Fischer's group is trying to do—spread the message about God. Would their knowledge of God change the Lessers' behavior?

Of course, not all Lessers are dangerous. Fischer and his family aren't, and what about Jamie? She isn't violent. She can't help it that she's a Lesser. Being one in and of itself doesn't make her violent and lawless. What if that's how it is with most Lessers, at least in the beginning? What if it's only later that they realize there is no hope for them?

My eyes fall on another part of the letter. *You've never heard of heaven or hell.* I've never heard these words, except "hell" as a curse. It's not used in a good way. Is it a real place? I feel like I'm going to be sick.

I tear the paper to shreds and take it downstairs to burn. If anyone found it in my possession, I could be arrested. I don't think they would let me off as easily as the last time.

I watch the paper burn, but I can see the words as clearly as if they were printed in my brain. I'm glad. I don't want to forget them, not ever. I'm not entirely sure I believe them, but in case they're true, I want to remember.

35

It's a few days before my Test. My stomach protests at the thought. I no longer want to be whatever *they* will make me. I don't want to work in the government or for the Greaters. The only thing I look forward to about Test day is Keegan's return. So much has changed in the last three weeks, and I ache for something familiar. I miss Keegan's silly jokes and our easy companionship. I miss my friend.

Still, I feel anxious at his homecoming. Will he visit Mom? Will he mention her? Will he only talk about Greaters? Will he understand the changes in me?

At school I scrawl a half-hearted speech about all we've learned over the years and how proud we should be of each other and ourselves for making it as far as we have. It's pathetically short, but that's because I refuse to mention our bright futures or the benefits we have as a society.

"What's that you're working on?" Mrs. Sewell asks.

"My speech." I want to draw the words back as soon as I say them. Mrs. Sewell thinks my speech was completed days ago.

"How's it coming?"

"Not as smoothly as I'd like."

She smiles. "I'm happy to take a look if you need me to."

"Thanks, Mrs. Sewell. I'm going to polish it a little

more."

It's a few minutes before class starts, and I put the paper away. I had hoped to talk to Ava before school, but so far, I haven't seen her. What's taking her so long? Class starts and she doesn't make it in time.

We go through the motions of the graduation ceremony again today. Why do we have to do it so often? How hard is it to walk down an aisle?

Finally, school lets out, still with no sign of Ava. Worry settles in my gut, and I'm surer than ever that I want to talk to her.

Instead of going straight to the hospital, I go to Ava's. She could have spent the day outside of Markus' room, but she might be home sick.

No one answers at her house, and I knock several times. I press my nose against a window off her front porch, but the drapes are drawn like they were a few days ago. I let out a sigh and start to the hospital. Is Markus out of his isolation? Maybe Ava's family has finally been allowed to visit.

How would that work, if he really has seen something he shouldn't? Can they erase his memory? The thought gives me chills, even in the heat. What exactly can the Greaters do, and how far will they go?

The second floor is busier than usual. Medics scurry back and forth between rooms as I head toward Markus's.

The door hangs open, and I stop and stare. Has Ava's family been allowed in after all this time?

But as I near the door I see I'm wrong. The room has been gutted. The bed has no sheets, the room has no other furniture, and the windows are open to let in fresh air and light. There's a sole occupant in the room, and he's bent over scrubbing something in the floor.

"What's going on? Did they move Markus to another room?"

The cleaning man looks up and shrugs. His appearance stops me in my tracks. His cheeks are hollow, and his eyes sunk in. He looks like he hasn't eaten in days. "I can't give information on the patients, ma'am."

It hits me then, why he looks so terrible. He's a Lesser. He must be! He must be safe or they wouldn't let him out of the Lesser city, but terror worms its way down my back.

I force myself to calm down. Fischer was a Lesser. How would he treat this man? The answer comes almost immediately.

"Thanks," I say, doing my best to smile, and I hurry from the room. Markus is gone. Ava is gone. Their house is empty. What happened to them?

I head to the stairs and jog up two at a time. Fischer might know something—anything—even if it's only an idea. He's sitting behind his computer, and I lean on the counter in front of him. "Ava's gone," I whisper.

He glances up from the screen. His eyes are clear, and he doesn't seem surprised. "Yes?"

"So is Markus."

He glances around, and then his eyes land back on me. "You know I can't talk about other patients, Hana."

"Ava isn't a patient, and I'm not asking you to tell me specifics. I want to know your theories."

He leans back and sighs. "Ava's been on a lot of pills lately."

What does that have to do with anything?

"Once you're hooked, you're not much good for

anything else. Where do they send people who aren't helping society progress?"

My heart stops for a fraction of a second, and then it restarts at triple speed.

"They made her a Lesser?" It comes out in a shocked, tiny whisper. My two friends are gone. And then I think of Markus. "Him too, right?"

Fischer glances around again and shrugs. "Medical allowances run out, Hana."

Is he trying to tell me something? If so, I can't think of what it might be. My throat feels like it's swelling shut, and I swallow hard. They're making everyone around me Lessers, and I don't understand why. Has this happened in the past? If so, why haven't I heard about it before? Why is it happening now?

Fischer puts his hand on my arm. It's warm and soft. He gives a tight squeeze, and then lets go quickly. It's enough to get my attention, though. He's never touched me like this before. I wasn't prepared for the way my skin would tingle, or the way it would make my heart skip.

"Don't think about it right now," he says. "Go see your mom. She's waiting on you."

I know he's right, but I feel frozen in place. "Do you know these things for sure, or are they only theories?" I feel like I need to know this.

"They're theories. I stop by the second floor every day on my way in, just to see what I can find. I never find anything, but today I found an empty room. I put two and two together."

I nod and push off the counter. Maybe he's wrong. Maybe we're both wrong. "OK."

My mom is asleep when I get to her room. The lights are off, and the room seems unbearably dark and gloomy. I sit in a chair beside the bed, and that's when I notice a paper sticking out of Mom's book. It's like a page marker.

I pull it out and read. *"For God so loved the world that He gave His only begotten Son, that whosoever believeth in Him should not perish, but have everlasting life."*

I suck in air so quickly I choke on it. A glass of water sits on the bedside table and I grab it and gulp.

What are these words? Why are they in Mom's book? I scan them again and can't believe what I'm seeing.

What do the words mean? God loves the world. He has a Son? That seems strange. I've never heard of this Son before, but apparently God gave up His Son, so that whoever believed in Him wouldn't perish. Whoever believed in Him would have eternal life.

My mind whirls. I really can't make sense of these words. Did Fischer leave this for me? Or is the paper really and truly Mom's? I'm afraid to bring it up, in case it gets her in trouble, but I don't want to just take it.

My mom's chest rises and falls as she takes a deep, rattling breath.

Watching her makes my nose and eyes burn. My mom is sick. She's really, really sick. She thinks she's going to die.

The realization hits me in the stomach and causes so much pain I wish it were me instead. I have terrible, wretched, unforgivable thoughts. Why couldn't it be Dad? Or Jamie's mom? After all, she gave up her own daughter to the Greaters. Why Mom?

Does anyone have an answer to that question?

Does God? Does He have a reason behind Mom's

illness?

If He does, then I hate Him.

As soon as the thought comes I dismiss it. If there is a God, He is the only one who can help Mom.

I don't hate Him. I need Him.

I make a split decision and shove the paper in my bag. I want these words. I crave these words. I'm obsessed with these words.

I don't mention them when Mom wakes up, and neither does she.

36

"Can we talk?" I whisper to Fischer.

He's about to take a glass of water to someone, but he stops for me. "What is it?"

I glance around, and then show him the paper. "This was in my mom's book. Did you put it there?"

His eyes widen and he shoves the paper back in my bag. Water trickles down the glass as he sets it on the counter, and he takes my arm and walks me to the stairs.

I should be thinking about the words on that paper, or Mom, or anything—but I'm not. I'm only thinking how this is the second time today Fischer has touched me. Tingles race down my arm all the way to my fingertips.

"I didn't put it there." He lets go and I feel the absence of his hand like the absence of the sun.

"Then who did?"

"I don't know." He runs a hand through his hair, a frown on his face.

Obviously, he doesn't like not knowing something of this magnitude.

"What are these words?" I ask.

"It's part of the Bible. It's called a Bible verse."

"A Bible verse? Like poetry?"

He gives me a half smile and shrugs. "Exactly like poetry, only much more truthful and important."

I run the words through my mind again, and my

throat feels tight with emotion. "Can you explain it to me?" Does Mom understand it? Has she even read it? She did want to know what happens to her when she dies. I swallow back my tears.

Fischer doesn't hesitate, and his eyes are soft and understanding. "Yes, I would love to explain it to you, but I can't do it here."

"My house, tonight," I say before I can change my mind. If I could get away with talking to Easton in the middle of the night then I can get away with talking to Fischer. "Can you come?"

"Are you sure?" His eyes watch me as if he's studying me, gauging how serious I am.

"Yes," I say.

"Then I'll be there."

Dr. Lane comes around the corner and smiles at me. "Hi, Hana. Did you see your mom?"

"I did," I say with a wave. "I'll see you later."

Fischer holds the door for me, and I slip away without another word.

I act as normal as possible when Dad comes home. He acts short with me. Frustrated. He's obviously thinking of last night, and trying to gauge whether or not I was actually doing something I shouldn't be.

Minutes pass like hours as I wait for dark, and then bedtime, and then much, much later than bedtime.

Finally, I tiptoe downstairs to wait for the knock that will come. I'm tempted to peek out the window or even step outside, but the thought of a guard seeing me stops me.

Just when I think I can't wait a moment longer, he comes.

"Sorry it took me so long. There are more guards

than usual." He's wearing a black hoodie, and he pulls it away from his face. A brown curl falls in his eye, and I want to push it away for him.

I don't.

"Are you OK?" I ask. I know how it feels to run from guards.

"Yeah, they didn't see me."

I don't want to admit how glad I am. What if he were to get caught? What if he were to get sent away, too? Every friend I have would be gone. I sit on a stool and pat the seat beside me. "My dad's asleep. Whisper, please."

He grins. "I can do that." He pulls something from a bag slung over his shoulder. I recognize it right away, because I've seen it before, in the box of recovered books from the Baily's Book Store.

"A Bible," I say.

He nods. "That's right. The verse you found is from John chapter three, verse sixteen." He flips it open and finds the page he's looking for. *"For God so loved the world that He gave His only begotten Son that whosoever believeth in Him should not perish but have everlasting life."*

I read the words to myself, running over them again and again. "So God gave us His son, to trade for our everlasting life?" I ask. "It's kind of like our allowances. We give up a food allowance to pay for food. Only God paid that price for us. He gave up His son to pay for everlasting life."

Fischer's eyes light up with excitement. "Exactly." He leans closer and lowers his voice. "God made this world, Hana. He made you and me, and the trees and the birds. He made it all! And He gave us a choice whether or not to follow him. He loves us, though, and hopes we'll choose to go with Him."

I force my mind away from the feelings I get from hearing Fischer say my name. He says it softly, reverently. I like it.

"But what's the alternative?" I ask. For Mom's sake I have to find out. "What happens if we don't have this everlasting life?"

"It's talking about heaven," Fischer says. "Everlasting life in heaven. When you die you'll either go there or hell. With God, you'll go to heaven."

There are those words—heaven and hell. That's what Mr. Elders mentioned in his letter.

"Heaven and hell are places?"

"Yeah, they are."

Now I feel silly, like I should have known this all along. "Oh. So what's hell?"

He opens his mouth to speak, but then snaps it shut. His shoulders sag and he sighs. "I don't think I'm qualified for this explanation. You need to meet the others. Mr. Elders has been leading others to God for most of his life. He'll know what to tell you."

I bite my lip. "How do I meet him?" I keep thinking of the market, and the park. I don't want to do that again. I want to meet someone where we can talk freely. Maybe then I'll learn something new.

He watches me, thinking. "I meet with them on Sunday nights. Eleven o'clock. Can you come?"

More lip biting. The last time I sneaked out didn't end so well, but I'm more determined this time, and I can be more careful. "I can come. Just tell me where."

"Down by the river, in the abandoned riverboat."

There used to be a lot of riverboats, or so I've heard. Now there's just the one. I thought it was condemned and deemed unsafe, but maybe I'm wrong.

"Isn't it dangerous by the river? It seems kind of open to scrutiny."

"Trust me." He pushes the Bible toward me. "Do you want to borrow this?"

Is he serious? "Yes!" I tuck the Bible under my robe.

He smiles. "I'm glad you're coming, Hana." He pauses like he wants to say something else, but he doesn't. "See you later."

"Tomorrow," I say. "I'll see you tomorrow at the hospital."

"Right. Goodnight." He steps outside and I close the door softly behind him. I can't help it, I watch him through the window to make sure he gets away safely.

I turn around to go to bed, and I freeze.

My dad sits on the bottom step, an expectant look on his face. "Care to tell me what that was all about?"

37

"Were you getting another drink of water?" he says sarcastically. "You've been awfully thirsty these last two nights."

I'm not sure, but I think he's asking me to just say yes. He doesn't really want to believe I'm doing anything I shouldn't be doing.

I shrug, not wanting to lie but not wanting to tell the truth.

"I saw someone leave. Who was it?"

I step away from the door nervously, even though I'm sure Fischer is gone. Is it wrong to lie to Dad? Somehow I get the feeling it is. I just don't want to get Fischer in trouble.

When he realizes I'm not going to answer, he moves toward the window and looks into the backyard. "Hana, you've got to stop this. Whatever you're doing has to stop. I won't be able to save you if they get it in their heads you're a rebel." His voice is angry, frustrated.

"I'm only trying to help Mom," I say. And it's true. She wants to know about God as much as I do.

He shakes his head. "She can't be helped, Hana. I wish she could, and if there was a way, we'd find it. But there's not!" Anger smolders behind his eyes. "You have to stop. You're a few days from your Test, and then you'll start your training. I always thought I'd be sad to see you go, but now I think it will be the best thing for you."

His words sting. Does he want me to go away? Rejection and anger boil in my gut. "I'm going to bed, Dad. Goodnight."

He grabs my arm. "You're lucky I don't go right now and turn you in myself. Your actions are against the law, and they could come back to hurt our whole family."

Betrayal feels exactly like icy water being dumped down your back in the snow, at the same time as someone punching you in the gut. You have no chance of breathing.

He wants to turn me in? He's no better than Jamie's mom, but at least he's not doing it. Yet.

Suddenly I remember Lilith's words to me at school a few days ago. She said I better not do something that was going to reflect badly on everyone. Is that what she's afraid of, too? That if the Greaters suspect there are too many law breakers there will be repercussions?

"I know the law, Dad," I say, shrugging out of his hold. It's the best I can give him.

His thin lips tell me he's not happy, but he doesn't stop me from going up the stairs this time.

I get in bed and contemplate Sunday night. The night before my Test. Two nights from now. What will I find down by the river? Words like God, heaven, and hell swirl through my head. Words so foreign to me, and yet Fischer knew all about them.

Is it true? Is there really such a thing as God? Are there real places called Heaven and Hell? Is this where we go when we die?

Most of all, why don't the Greaters want us to know about them?

Mr. Elders's letter comes back to me. The Greaters knew some of their laws wouldn't be followed if the people had another authority — the Bible.

I remember Mrs. Baily. She had known what she held in her hands that day at the bookstore, and she was afraid of it. Did she know why? Was her fear only that it was outlawed, and she wanted to burn it as soon as possible? Or did she know the truths the book contained, and feared I would turn her in?

There aren't any answers to my questions, of course. I'm beginning to get used to that feeling.

The Bible lays hidden under my mattress. I'm tempted to bring it out and read it, but Dad might be staying awake to keep an eye on me. Would he turn me in if he found that Bible?

Maybe I'll get a chance to read it tomorrow.

I'm too excited for Sunday night at eleven o'clock. I toss and turn in bed, willing the morning to come. Finally, I drift into a light sleep, but not before remembering Ava and Markus, and wondering where they've gone.

School on Friday is loud. Most of the kids can't wait for the one month summer break, but the others, the ones like me who are testing on Monday, are quiet. Nervous. Contemplative. There are fifty-one of us, in all — or fifty, now that Jamie's gone.

I wander the halls alone. The day seems empty, and the final lessons are pointless. I should try to listen, but I don't. My mind drifts with each new face I see. Have any of them heard about God? Are their parents part of this underground movement? Do they know others who have been sent away?

I can't tell for sure, but I doubt it. None of them are restless like I am. None of them look scared, or confused, or like they're feeling all of the feelings I do.

"How's your mom?"

The question jolts me out of my musings. "What?"

Lilith stands in front of me, a strange expression, almost like a smile, on her face. "Your mom. Is she OK?" She blushes a little and starts intertwining her fingers like she's nervous just speaking to me. "I heard my parents talking about it, and I was just hoping she was OK. I didn't realize she was so bad off."

"Your parents were talking about it?" Why would her parents be thinking about Mom being sick? Lilith's dad works for the head of the city. Do the city leaders always know who is sick? And then talk about it around the dinner table?

She looks away, and then down at her shoes. I've definitely made her uncomfortable. "I'm sorry, Hana. I shouldn't have brought it up. It's just that I know you've been alone a lot, with your mom sick, and Jamie gone. I just wanted you to know you have a friend if you need one. I can just tell there's something different going on. I don't know." She takes a step away. "Anyway, I'm really sorry."

My mind spins with this new information. Lilith has never, not once, been nice to me. "Lilith!"

She pauses and turns to me expectantly.

"Thank you. I'll remember that, if I need a friend."

She smiles and walks toward her next class.

I can tell there's something different going on.

What was that supposed to mean? So her parents talking about Mom is out of the ordinary, and Jamie and Ava being sent away is not the norm. And other people are noticing. I'm not sure I can trust her, but for now, I'll take what support I can get.

I hurry to my next class, more anxious than ever to

see Fischer at the hospital.

38

"She's worse, isn't she?" I ask. Fischer stands outside of Mom's room after school. Another medic stands with him, and the door to the room is closed.

Fischer's eyes are soft and kind. "Yes."

His one word sends fear into my stomach that immediately takes root and begins to fester. It burns and bubbles and I want to throw up. "What happened?"

"She started vomiting this morning. She hasn't been able to keep anything down, not even water."

"Why don't they help her?" I ask too loudly.

The other medic seems surprised at my forcefulness. She glances between Fischer and me, her expression wary.

"We're doing what we can," he says. "Trust us, Hana."

He says it in his normal, kind and caring voice. I do trust him, and it calms me.

"Would you like some water?" the other medic asks.

I wouldn't, but I'd rather be alone with Fischer. "Sure, thanks."

She hurries away.

"Fischer, what are they doing for her?" I step toward him.

He shakes his head. "Giving her medicine to help her not throw up, but it's not helping. She won't eat, not that she could if she tried. I'm really sorry, Hana."

I look over his shoulder at a window leading out to the city. I can't believe this is happening. This can't be real. My mom is safe at the military school, in the middle of a lecture. I'm at home with Jamie, and we're going over my speech for the hundredth time. I'm not here. She's not here, in this hospital.

"Hana, would you like to come in?" It's Dr. Lane, and she's holding the door open for me.

I push past Fischer and lean over Mom's shivering form. "Hi, Mom."

She tries to move her head, but it's too hard for her. She moves her eyes to me instead. "Hi, Hana." She attempts a smile but fails miserably. "You don't have to stay and see this."

I sit beside the bed and take her hand. "Of course I'm staying." I'm not sure, but I think she's glad. Her body seems to relax, and she closes her eyes.

Dr. Lane smiles at me and leaves the room quietly.

I know the truth now. My mom is going to die. I don't know when. I don't know who's to blame. Who knows if the chemo drugs would have helped? Stories from the Early Days say sometimes they didn't work.

Regardless, the doctors had the power to try, and they didn't.

I'm angry with them, but more than that I'm devastated.

My mom seems to have fallen asleep. Her chest rises and falls softly.

I lean my head on the bedrail as tears drip from my eyes. Sobs rack my body and I try to keep still, but I can't.

I suddenly remember the Bible verse in my bag and I pause. That strip of paper belongs to Mom.

Obviously, she needs it. I gently pull my hand away from hers and dry my face on my sleeve. The paper is at the bottom of the bag, and I pull it out and lay it under the book on her bedside table.

Who cares if anyone sees it now? What more could they do to her?

The minutes tick by. Tick, tick, tick. Every one gives me one extra second with her. Every tick lets me see her for one more moment. I don't hate the ticks. I don't resent the time spent watching her sleep. Instead, I relish it.

"How is she?" Fischer asks, popping his head in.

"Sleeping."

"Are you cold? I can bring you a blanket."

I hadn't realized it, but I'm actually freezing. "Yeah, that would be great."

He steps out and returns a moment later with a blanket. I reach for it, but he shakes his head and wraps it around my shoulders.

"How much longer, do you think?" I ask. It's so very hard to ask, but I'd rather know.

"I don't know, Hana. From my training, I'd say soon, but I've never actually dealt with the mutation before. Dr. Lane might know more."

I nod, accepting his answer. Soon. "She needs to know about everlasting life." The words feel strange in my mouth, but I don't know how else to say it. "What's going to happen to her? She was asking me just the other day."

"I'll make sure she knows, Hana. If she wants to know I'll tell her."

My heart nearly bursts with gratitude. "You'll tell her?" It comes out in a breathy, pathetic cry. "What if you get in trouble?"

He laughs softly. "I don't care if I get caught. That's what I'm here to do—spread the news."

I frown. "What do you mean, that's what you're here to do?"

"It's the only reason I tested, Hana. To come to a Middle city and start a revolution."

39

My mouth drops open and I stare at him. "What are you talking about, Fischer? What kind of revolution?"

He pulls the empty chair close to mine and leans in. "People are dying every day, Hana. They're dying and they're going to hell. Not because they're bad people, but because they don't know there even *is* a hell! Someone has to tell them, and we can't do that under our present government. There has to be a change. Someone has to tell them." His words are spoken slowly, softly, and yet I've never heard a more convincing speech ever.

I swallow down my confusion. "I have to be honest, Fischer. It doesn't make all that much sense to me."

"I know, but you'll understand more once you hear Mr. Elders speak."

"Can you tell me more about Heaven?"

His worried face falls away and is replaced with what can only be described as a glow—like someone who has a terrific secret and they're about to let you in on it. "Heaven? Heaven is spending an eternity with God."

I watch him, waiting for more. When he doesn't speak I look away. "Do you know what I've always been taught? About reincarnation, I mean?"

"Yes," he says. "I was taught the same thing at

school. It's a lie, though, all lies. Don't you see? It's natural for people to look for a deeper meaning. The Greaters had to give us something to believe."

His words make sense. After all, I've seen the deception in the city myself. I give a sharp nod. "OK, I believe you."

He smiles and stands. "I knew you would, Hana." He pauses, like he's going to say or do something else, but then he turns and leaves the room.

I stare after him for long moments, not sure what my feelings are. I want nothing more in this moment than for him to come back. Just to sit with me. Just to wait with me.

My mom wakes up minutes before I have to leave, and it's only because Dr. Lane has returned. I don't dare bring up heaven and hell with her in the room, so our talk will have to wait. I kiss Mom goodbye and head home.

The sun sinks lower in the sky, and with each step I take I feel like I've gained a hundred pounds. The past two nights of staying up late are catching up with me, and I'm anxious for a night of uninterrupted sleep.

I walk through the front door and freeze.

Keegan and his mom sit on our couch. My dad is in the armchair, smiling at me like he's just given me the biggest birthday present ever.

"Hana!" Keegan says. He flies off the couch and rushes to me.

At first I think he's going to hug me, which he's never done before, but he doesn't. He just stands in front of me smiling, all six foot two of him.

My throat swells up and tears burn my eyes. I try to laugh instead of cry. I'm not sure I've ever felt so much relief in my entire life. Keegan's here. A friend. A confidant. The familiar.

"You're early," is all I can manage to say around my tears. "I thought you weren't coming until Monday."

He grins. "I wanted to surprise you. I thought I could help take your mind off the Test."

I laugh, but truthfully, my mind hasn't been on the Test anyway. "I'm glad you're here, Keegan." And I mean it. I crane my neck around him to see his mom. "Hi, Mrs. Clem."

She waves her hand in a small circle. "Hi, Hana. I've missed seeing you."

I suddenly wonder why I haven't thought to visit her in these last weeks.

My dad stands up. "I've started a vegetable stew, Hana. Why don't you and Keegan set the table?"

"Sure," I say. "Let me put my bag upstairs."

Keegan moves to follow me.

I freeze on the stairs and stare at him in confusion. I don't understand what he's doing. Boys and girls aren't allowed to be alone.

He pauses and looks at me, still smiling, waiting for me to keep moving.

I glance at Dad and his mom, but they're talking again and not paying us any mind, so I keep moving toward my room. He follows.

"I made my mom keep it a secret," Keegan says. "With your mom and everything, I knew you'd probably like some extra cheering up. I almost asked Jamie to come over, but Mom said it'd be better with just us tonight."

I drop my bag onto my bed and stare at him in shock. "Your mom didn't tell you?"

He frowns for the first time. "Tell me what?"

A bark of a laugh escapes my lips, and I drop onto my bed like a bag of school books. I can't believe she didn't tell him. "Jamie was sent away."

"Sent away? What are you talking about?"

I look into his eyes and hate to be the one to break the news. No wonder his mom didn't mention it. "She got pregnant and refused to abort the baby, so the Greaters sent her to a Lesser city."

He stares at me like he's waiting for the punch line. He completely doesn't believe me. Finally, he shakes his head. "That can't be true, Hana. That doesn't happen."

I stand face to face with him now. "It does happen, Keegan, and it did. Jamie's not the only one. Do you remember Ava and Markus?"

"The twins? Markus used to play football with us after school. Sure, I remember them."

"Gone, both of them."

He's shaking his head again, but this time he looks a lot less sure of himself. "There has to be more to the story, Hana. They don't just send people away." Some emotion plays on his face, something I don't recognize. He wavers. "I've heard of others—"

My dad's voice drifts up to us, calling us to hurry and set the table.

I step close to Keegan. "There is definitely more to the story, Keegan, and I hope you'll help me find it."

He seems startled by my sudden closeness, and he steps away. "What do you mean?"

"A lot has changed since you left. *I've* changed." I pause and glance at my bedroom door to make sure no one is in the hallway listening. "Will you come with me Sunday night?"

"Sunday night? You mean after curfew?" His

eyebrows shoot up and his voice cracks.

I shrug. "Are you coming or not?"

He stares at me for what feels like forever. Finally, he nods. "Yeah, I guess so. Where are we going?"

This is the part I'm sure he's not going to like, and it's worse because I only have a moment to explain. "I've met some people," I say. "They've told me about God. A real God, not some imaginary being who lives in a cloud."

He laughs. "Very funny. Where are we going, for real?"

"I'm not joking, Keegan. You've been gone, and so maybe you don't understand how things feel around here. My mom is dying."

That shuts him up pretty fast.

"She wants to know what's going to happen to her, and so do I. I don't trust what the Greaters have taught us all these years."

"Why," he interrupts me. "What makes you doubt them on that subject?"

This is too big for a quick conversation, but I try. "They have medicine to heal her, but they're not giving it to her. I overheard the doctors discussing it when they didn't know I was there. And besides, they've obviously lied about other things."

His eyes widen. He takes a deep breath and wipes his hand down his face. "OK, so what? We're going to meet these people in the dead of the night?"

I can tell he thinks I will say no. "Exactly."

40

Keegan does a good job of keeping his face neutral when we go back downstairs. We set the table and have dinner together. My dad beams the whole time, and I wonder if it's because he thinks Keegan's presence will get me out of the funk I've been in.

"Won't you get in trouble for being over here after dark?" I ask, realizing the sun is setting fast.

"I think it will be OK, just this once," Mrs. Clem says with a smile.

"So Keegan," Dad says. "Tell us about Middle City 1."

Keegan's face lights up and he leans forward. "They have so many things I've never heard of there. It's a richer city, one that has more Greaters in it than our city. There are places called movie theaters, and they have something called ice cream. Everything looks newer, too. It isn't so run down and condemned."

"What's ice cream?" I ask.

"A dessert. It's like..." he thinks for a minute. "Frozen milk! I think that's what they called it. It's sweet, though, made with sugar. I can't even tell you how good it is. And the music system is amazing. They have these things called electric guitars. The instruments hook up to something called a speaker, and it makes the music louder, so more people can hear it."

The things he describes sound foreign to me. How can such advanced technology exist? But then I realize I've seen things in our own city—things like the guards' small computers, and the strange glasses one guard wore in the night. And, of course, the blinking lights.

"What's the training schedule like?" Dad asks. "And how do you move into the industry after you finish?"

I stare at Keegan while he talks. I'm so happy he's home. It's so normal. Nothing has been normal in a while. His face practically glows while he speaks, and his blue eyes are lit with excitement. He tells Dad about his usual daily schedule, and about how when he's finished training they'll test him on his skill level to see where he'll fit into the entertainment industry.

Way before I'm ready, it's time to say goodnight. Keegan lingers at the door after his mom hurries across the backyard to her house. My dad surprises me by going upstairs and leaving me alone with him.

Butterflies tickle my stomach as I look up at him. "I've missed you."

His eyes are gentle. "I've missed you, too."

We stand there like this for too long, and I need to make a move away. I step back. "Will you be at the graduation ceremony tomorrow?"

He gives a sad, lopsided smile. "I wouldn't miss it for the world."

We say goodnight and I hurry upstairs to bed. My heart is lighter than it has been in weeks, and I'm too excited to sleep, even if I'll regret staying up when morning comes. My eyes fall on the Bible Fischer gave me.

Fischer.

Confusion replaces the light feelings again. It's a feeling I'm getting more and more used to. If I can't sleep, I might as well read. I flip pages to the book of John, where Fischer read to me. I start reading, and I don't stop until I've devoured the whole book.

Goose bumps prick my arms as I read about this Man called God's son, who was born, lived, and then died. Jesus.

I suddenly forget all about Keegan and graduation and the Test. All I want to do is meet Mr. Elders. I want to know more. I may not be able to save Mom from the mutation, but at least I can help her learn about Heaven.

My eyes finally get too heavy to read, and I drift to sleep.

Morning comes, and I hurry to school. I wear something nice—a white skirt and blue blouse—just because it's graduation day. Jamie and I used to talk about what we'd wear for our last day of school.

It's the last day of school! I'm excited in spite of myself. Maybe it's because I have a secret, or maybe it's because Keegan is home. Whatever it is, I'm glad to feel happy.

The day passes in a blur of emotion. I miss Jamie, and I realize too late that Mom won't get to see me graduate. Tears start running as I study my speech.

Mrs. Sewell passes with an understanding smile. "Graduation is always an emotional day," she says.

But she can't possibly understand. For the first time, I wonder about Mrs. Sewell. She's as kind as Fischer. Maybe she's part of the rebellion, too. That thought makes me happy.

The small gymnasium is filled with family and friends at noon, and the other graduates line up around me. This is it.

"How are you?" Lilith asks.

Again I'm suspicious of her kind voice. Has she seen Keegan out there? Maybe she guessed he would be coming home, and she wants to be sure she makes a good impression. "I'm fine. How are you?"

"Excited. And nervous."

I smile at her and nod. "Yeah, that too."

"I was thinking that maybe we could hang out sometime. Maybe we could be friends."

This is the most shocking thing I've ever heard her say. Is she serious?

Someone gives the cue, and it's time to start marching. I only have time to smile and nod, and we start into the gym. People cheer and clap as each graduate receives a diploma. My stomach does summersaults as I give my speech.

Before I know it the service is over. My dad hugs me, his smile as big as the sun. "Your mom and I are so proud of you."

I look to his eyes, needing to see that he means it.

His eyes glow with tears. Maybe he is proud, after all. A small piece of my world fits back into place.

I've gotten through the first big hurdle of the weekend—graduation. Tomorrow I'll meet Fischer's group, and on Monday I'll take my Test. I dread it all and yet, I can't wait to get it over with.

As we're leaving the school, I spot Easton. He leaves the graduation ceremony alone. His shoulders slump and he shuffles like he's lost his best friend. I know exactly how he feels.

41

Sunday is sunny and warm, making for the most perfect day ever.

"Why don't you spend the afternoon with Keegan?" Dad says over breakfast. "We can go together to see your mom, and then I'll stay when you leave to meet him."

I stare at him, unsure if he's implying what I think he's implying.

He smiles, like he can read my mind. "I've already talked to Margaret about it, and she agreed to chaperone you."

Relief floods me, and I nod. "That sounds great, Dad. Thanks." Having Mrs. Clem there makes it better. For some reason I'm afraid to be alone with Keegan. What will he expect from me? I'm still not sure he'll like the new me, once he gets to know her.

My dad smiles, all signs of his frustration and anger a few days ago gone now.

We head to the hospital after breakfast. My mom looks as bad today as she did two days ago. She's as skinny as a skeleton, and dark circles ring her eyes.

"There's my graduate," she says. "How did it go?"

"OK." I bend down to give her a kiss, and her cheek burns my lips. "Mom, you've got a fever."

She shrugs. "It can't be helped."

I grind my teeth and lean away. There is help, and I want to tell her all about the Bible Fischer brought me, but that's not an option with Dad sitting there.

"Tell me about the ceremony," she says.

This is something I can discuss. "It was short, thankfully, and my speech seemed to go over well."

"It was great!" Dad says. "The people clapped for her like you've never heard."

My mom practically beams. "How did Jamie do?"

Pain stabs at my gut, but I recover quickly. "She did great." I glance at Dad, but he doesn't acknowledge my statement.

"That's good. I'm so proud of you, Hana. I wish I could have been there."

"I know, Mom. I wish you could have been there, too."

"Keegan's in town," Dad says. "He got in the night before last."

My mom's face lights up a little more, or as much as it can. "Keegan? Tell him to come see me. I'd love to talk to him." When she finishes talking, she takes a deep breath and closes her eyes.

"Mom, just rest. We'll sit here with you."

She doesn't respond, and I wonder if she's already asleep.

I meet Keegan and Mrs. Clem just before lunch. We agree to use some of our entertainment allowances to eat at the small restaurant near The Shops. We visit Baily's Bookstore after we eat. Mr. Baily runs the store today, and he smiles and waves at us as we browse.

"How many books have you read since I left?" Keegan asks. "Remember you said you would read at least ten books while I was gone? One for every month I was away."

I smile at the childish promise. "I think I fell a little short."

After the bookstore we visit the apothecary, and I show Mrs. Clem the new soaps made from flowers.

After that we head to the park to watch the kids play.

All of our talk centers on Keegan and his training, which suits me fine. I can't say anything important in front of Mrs. Clem anyway.

We say goodbye at supper time, and Mrs. Clem wishes me well on my Test.

"I'll see you later," Keegan says.

I watch his eyes, and then nod once. "Right. I'll see you later."

I get to work on supper, and Dad comes home from the hospital. His shoulders sag and he sits on the couch with a sigh. "Your mom said to tell you she loves you, and she's sorry she fell asleep."

"Did you tell her not to apologize for that? I know she can't help it."

"I did, but she feels bad anyway."

Of course she does. But I can tell something's wrong, because Dad looks like he's been in a fight, at least emotionally. "What's wrong, Dad?"

He takes a long time to answer. When he does, he looks at me with sad, sorrowful eyes. "She was doing worse. A lot worse."

That's all he needs to say. My happy afternoon fades away and is replaced with sadness.

We eat in silence, and I tell him I'm tired and head to my room. I'm anxious for the night to come, and I watch my clock for each passing moment. Around nine o'clock I hear Dad close his bedroom door. An hour passes. Finally, it's time to head outside.

Fog blankets the ground, which makes it all the scarier when Keegan slides up beside me in the darkness.

"Are you sure about this?" he asks.

"Yeah, pretty sure."

"We don't have to go, you know."

I'm not sure why he's trying to talk me out of it, but after the last three weeks, it kind of annoys me. "I'm going with or without you, Keegan. I would like to go with you, though." And it's true. I want Keegan to hear this message as well—after all, I love him. What kind of person would I be if I didn't share it with him? Besides, I'm excited to have him with me, period.

"All right, all right. I'm coming," he says. I imagine his grimace and sagging shoulders in the dark, because I'm sure that's what he's doing.

The thought makes me smile. "I'm glad you're home, Keegan."

He pauses, but then he nudges me forward. "Me, too. Now let's get moving before someone catches us."

I start walking and I know I should be quiet, I mean, I *really* know it—I've been caught twice past curfew, and a third time will probably get me in major trouble—but I've missed him and so I keep talking.

"You've learned to break a few rules yourself," I say, thinking of his nudge, and how he came to my room with me the night he came home.

"Yeah, I guess so, but it's only harmless stuff. Nothing to get me arrested."

His words remind me that he doesn't know everything that's gone on in the last few weeks. What will he think when he learns I *was* arrested? I don't want him to know, and for a moment I wish the arrest and everything leading up to it had never happened. I miss the happy life we used to have. I miss the promising, innocent me that I used to be.

We hurry through backyards, making our way to the levies and then the river's edge beyond. The summer is quickly approaching and this works to our advantage. There are no leaves to crackle, and soft grass has sprouted everywhere.

"You never did tell me where we're going," he says.

I stop when I come to the street we'll have to cross. "The riverboat."

"What did you say?"

I peek out into the dark street and glance both ways. It looks empty. "That's exactly what I said, but Fischer told me it was safe."

Keegan is standing close to me. I'm not sure if he's looking for protection, or if he's trying to protect me. Either way, he's close enough that I see his frown, even in the dark. "Who's Fischer?"

"He's a medic at the hospital," I say, glancing at the road again. I feel a little like I'm back at the guard station being questioned about breaking curfew. I don't want to talk about Fischer with Keegan.

"We need to cross now." I bolt into the street and make it to the other side in seconds, but when I look back I see Keegan is still standing in the shadows. What's the problem? Then I catch a movement at the corner. A guard has turned onto the street, and is moving through the fog, coming our way. He's on Keegan's side of the street.

I slip behind a tree, thankful for my black clothing. I can just barely see Keegan do the same.

My heart thumps so loud, I'm sure the guard can hear it. I keep swallowing like I haven't had anything to drink in weeks. What if Keegan gets caught? It would be all my fault.

The guard is in no hurry. Step, step, step.

Finally he passes Keegan. He doesn't even glance in Keegan's direction.

When the coast is clear, Keegan shoots across the street. He grabs my hand and we head toward the levies. It feels strange, his hand in mine. I've never held hands with anyone. His is warm and soft, and it feels like it's swallowing mine.

I almost pull away, but I can't bring myself to do it. It would hurt him, and he trusts me tonight. I just don't know what I'm supposed to feel. On top of everything else going on, the last thing I need is boy trouble.

The levies rise up in front of us like mountains, and we quickly jog to the top.

I stop and stare.

The riverboat is at the bottom of the levy and along the bank, but that's not what has me stopped. The lights are back. High in the sky, and far in the distance, they blink. Blink. Blink.

"Do you see that?" I ask. Somehow I'd forgotten about the blinking lights in the sky.

Keegan doesn't answer, and so I glance at him. He's staring, his face registering confusion and shock. "It is—flying?"

"I don't know, but I've seen it once before."

He breaks away from the flying lights long enough to look at me. "When?"

"A few weeks ago. I was out looking for Jamie." Sharp stabs poke at my stomach when I say her name. "We have a lot to catch up on, but I hope this meeting will explain at least a little of it."

Keegan doesn't say anything to that. We watch the blinking lights for one last moment, and then we start down the hill.

The riverboat is condemned, just like the rest of the riverfront area. Places like the Arch are crumbling, and pose a safety hazard to anyone who gets close. The guards warn us about the dangers regularly, to keep us from playing in them and getting hurt.

Is the boat really safe? Besides that, there is no electricity on the riverboat, and even if there were, we couldn't use it in the middle of the night. The guards would spot the lights and we would be caught. How are we going to communicate in a rickety old boat?

We sneak toward the river. A soft splashing sound comes from the water as fish jump at water bugs.

The misty fog is much worse at the water's edge, and I can barely see Keegan's form beside me. We climb the plank to the door of the boat and pause. Not a sound comes from inside.

Keegan looks at me and gives my hand a squeeze. "Are you ready?"

I swallow hard and give a sharp nod. "As ready as I'll ever be."

42

I try the knob but it's locked. That's no surprise since the riverboat's not used and has been condemned.

"Knock," says Keegan.

I tap lightly, hoping there aren't any guards nearby. Water laps around the ancient boat in the eerie darkness. It makes a splash. Splash. Splash.

The door slides open after only a second, and we step inside.

Blackness surrounds us, darker than the night outside. I stumble around in the inky room when someone gently takes my arm. "This way, Hana." It's Fischer, and I exhale in relief.

"Who's this?" another voice demands.

"Get the door shut and then ask questions," a third voice says. I recognized the voice as Mr. Elders.

How many people are on this boat? I suddenly feel frightened and claustrophobic. Fears race through my head. Maybe I shouldn't have brought Keegan. What if we're in danger? How well do I really know Fischer?

A lamp flickers on and the room is bathed in yellow, artificial light. A few men and women sit in old chairs, and Mr. Elders stands at the head of the group. Fischer still holds my arm, and a big guy holds Keegan back.

"Who are you?" the man growls.

Keegan holds his arms up, glancing around like a trapped animal.

"I brought him," I say quickly. "I didn't know that would be a problem."

"It's not," says Fischer. "It's OK."

The big man glances at Mr. Elders, who nods his head. "It's fine. Let him go, Vin."

Vin lets him go, but scowls at him. "Don't try anything funny."

Fischer tugs on my elbow. "Sorry about that. We typically know exactly who's coming, so there aren't any surprises. Come sit down."

I begin to follow him to my chair but then a thought hits me. "How do you have lights?" Fear digs its claws into my chest and my breathing stops. The guards are going to spot us.

"It's called a generator," Mr. Elders says. "It's from the Early Days, but it still works. It runs on gasoline."

"But won't the guards see the lights?" Keegan asks. His voice sounds a little panicked.

"Take a look at the windows, genius," Vin says.

Thick black material covers the windows. "Do they keep the light in?" I ask.

"That's right," Mr. Elders says. "They're called black out curtains, and they're from the Early Days, too." He steps forward. "My name is Jim Elders. It's nice to finally meet you, officially."

He's holding his hand out, so of course I take it. I smile. "It's nice to meet you, too."

"Who did you bring with you, Hana?"

"This is my friend, Keegan. He lives beside me. He's training in another city, but he came home on break. I thought this was an important message to share with my friends." I'm rambling and so I shut up.

"You're very right. It is important." He steps back to the front of the group. "We're all here now, and so we'll begin. Does anyone have questions?"

"How do you know the Bible is true?" The question is from a girl in the back. This must be a type of orientation meeting. Everyone here is new and learning.

"We take it by faith," says Mr. Elders. He explains about creation and how God made the world, and he talks about heaven and hell.

Fischer talked about God making everything, so the concept isn't totally new to me. I glance at Keegan. He's frowning, his eyebrows pulled close together.

I watch his face, anxious for this to make sense to him. It seems more real that way, more concrete. If someone else from my world can mesh with this new concept, then maybe it's actually true.

Keegan nods as Mr. Elders speaks, and I relax.

Mr. Elders goes on. "Jesus is God's son, and He volunteered to be the sacrifice for us, so that we don't have to go to hell. His blood for ours."

Tiny chill bumps prick my arms and I shiver.

"He came to this earth and lived as a human, and He was eventually killed. When his blood was spilled, our bonds were broken. We no longer had to go to hell to pay for our sins; we just had to go to Jesus. All we have to do is accept that gift of salvation."

These words play through my mind in a swirl of confusion. This Jesus, the son of God, died to pay for my wrong doing. "Why would He do that?"

Mr. Elders's face smooths into a happy and peaceful expression. "Because He loves us. His love is all encompassing and perfect. He loves us like no human has ever loved."

A burning fire starts in my chest and spreads down my arms, to my stomach and all the way down to my toes. I can't fathom someone loving me when He doesn't even know me. My dad's ready to give me up, and he's had me my whole life.

Some of the others start talking, and Keegan leans close to me. "I'm not sure I believe all of this."

The fire in my bones fizzles out. "What do you mean?"

"I'm not sure. I have to think about it all."

"But what if it's true?" I ask. Panic rises in my chest at the thought of him not believing. I need this to be real. It *must* be real.

Fischer lays his hand on my arm. "You didn't believe at first either, Hana. Everyone needs time to think it through. It's an unknown concept."

Keegan hasn't been upset about any of this—not the journey here, or getting pushed around by Vin, or being told he was destined for hell. But now he's glaring at Fischer's hand on my arm. "Who are you?" he asks.

"This is Fischer," I say. "He's the medic from the hospital. He takes care of my mom."

Some of the fire leaves his eyes, but he doesn't stop watching Fischer. "You're the one who told her about all of this?"

Fischer nods. "That's right."

"How do I know she can trust you?"

"Keegan please. I believe this. I do." I turn to Fischer. "What do I do now? Mr. Elders said something about accepting a gift."

"That's right," Fischer says. "You pray to God and tell Him you accept His payment. Tell Him you know you've sinned, and the price for that sin is hell. You tell

Him you're sorry for that sin, and you accept His gift of salvation from hell."

Fischer had mentioned prayer that day we spent together at the levies. He'd said they prayed before each meal. "What does pray mean?" I ask.

His eyebrows shoot up. "Pray? It just means to talk to God. We usually bow our heads and close our eyes, just to show our reverence to God. And then we talk to Him."

"You just talk to Him? Just like that?"

"I can help you," Fischer says. He bows his head and closes his eyes, and then words a simple prayer. I follow him bit by bit. My ears burn and my heart races. Is anyone looking at me? But when I finish I'm glad I did it. I'm more than glad. I'm thrilled!

"I have to tell my mom about this," I say quickly.

"She'll believe you, Hana. You can do it."

Tears fill my eyes in a flash. I'm so thankful for his words I want to hug him. I can't do that, so I talk instead. "I read part of the Bible you gave me. I've never seen anything like it."

"I know what you mean," Fischer says with a lopsided smile.

Keegan doesn't say anything, just listens. I want to know what's going on in his head, what he's thinking. I don't ask though. He's been gone a long time, and we've both changed in that time apart. I'm not sure he still wants me probing around in his head.

The other conversations quiet down, and someone speaks up. "I saw the lights in the sky again."

I spin around to see the speaker. It's a boy no older than I am. "I've seen them, too," I say. "I saw them a few weeks ago, and again tonight. What are the lights?"

Mr. Elders's face wrinkles up uncertainly. "That's a question that is a little harder to answer."

43

"We saw them a few weeks ago too," the boy says. "I was with my friend, and he fell out of the tree we were sitting in. He's been in the hospital ever since. Now his family is gone. Just gone!"

My mouth gapes open. "You were with Markus that night?"

He looks at me for the first time, and I realize I recognize him. He goes to my school. "We were just goofing off, climbing trees and stuff. We see these lights in the sky, and Markus falls right out of his tree and hits the ground. I didn't know what to do so I ran for help. The guard had me show her where Markus was, and told me to wait with her until backup came, but I ran away. I heard Markus, though. He asked her what the lights were."

That's why no one could see him. The thought sickens me. Whatever those lights are is a big secret, and the Greaters are willing to do whatever it takes to keep it.

"We believe the lights are a type of airplane," Mr. Elders says. "Airplanes were used in the Early Days to transport people from place to place, and sometimes they were used in wars. They fly in the air, like a giant, flying car. They take a lot of fuel to run, so the question is who is flying the airplane and why. Most likely it's the Greaters, but what are they doing, and why don't they want anyone to know?"

Keegan and I look at each other. He's frowning and his eyebrows are lowered. "The direction of the lights was west," he says. "Nothing is supposed to be out that way, but in Middle City 1, where I'm studying entertainment, there are jokes about a prison. They say it's where the Greaters send people who really make them mad. Supposedly, the Greaters have things grown and made, things like food, clothes, and furniture. No one takes it seriously, but they say it's in the west."

The thought that our own leaders have secret safe places, places kept from us and possibly for their good and no one else's, is disturbing.

"This is something I haven't heard," Mr. Elders says. "Thank you for sharing."

Glancing at Keegan, I try to assess how he's taking all of this. He's listened to everything that's been discussed, but he hasn't said much himself. He's obviously not sure about the possibility of God, but what does he think about learning the Greaters aren't what they seem?

The meeting ends and everyone takes turns leaving. Keegan and I get ready for our turn.

"I'll see you tomorrow," Fischer says. He glances at Keegan and then adds, "At the hospital when you visit your mom, I mean."

"Right, I'll see you then."

Tomorrow is my Test. I'll go first thing in the morning, and then go to the hospital to see her when I'm done. I can't wait to talk to her about God, and about salvation.

We bolt down the boardwalk and up the cobblestone pathway to the levies. A pang of loneliness hits me. I miss Mom more than words can ever express. Tears sting my eyes and I quickly wipe them away. The fog has gotten heavier since we were in the boat, and I need my eyes clear so I can see.

"Do you want me to go with you tomorrow?" Keegan asks quietly.

The grass at the levy is wet under my feet, and I slip. Keegan reaches to catch me so I don't go sliding down the hill. "Thanks," I say. We keep walking. "I would love for you to come. It's better than going alone or with all the other kids from school who are testing. I was supposed to be with Jamie." Saying her name sends another wave of loneliness washing over me.

"So it's true then, they really took her away."

"Of course, and Ava and Markus, too." I study him in the dark. I think of the information he offered up about the prison rumors. "Keegan, why are you willing to help Mr. Elders' people, if you don't believe in their cause?"

Emotions play across his face as we move onto the treed path back to our street. He shakes his head and frowns. "I don't believe what they say about God, but there were other things said in Middle City 1, stories about privileges the Greaters have that the rest of us don't have. I mostly ignored the rumors, but now I can see they might be more than rumors. Obviously the Greaters aren't what they appear to be. They're taking people from their homes and sending them away, they have secret flying machines and secret cities building them food, clothes, and who knows what else. They're refusing to give your mom the help she needs. Something's not right."

I shrug. "Technically the ones who were sent away broke the law. Jamie got pregnant, and Markus was out past curfew. Maybe Mom's medical allowance isn't enough to pay for chemo."

He shakes his head. "It still leaves the secret machine and city. That's not right." He frowns. "I've met a lot of Greaters since I've been away, and now I wonder how they all feel about this. Do they know it's going on? What are they told?"

His words settle on my shoulders. "You're right. I think we've only touched on the first clue of this mystery."

We're almost to our street now. The shady-treed path is all that separates us from our regular world. I'm not ready to go back yet. There's more to discuss. More to learn.

I turn to ask what others rumors he heard while he was away, but Keegan stops me and leans close. "That's not the only reason I'm helping though, Hana. I'm helping because it's important to you, and you are important to me. You know that, right?"

He's so close his warm breath tickles my face. My mind races, and yet the rest of my body is in slow motion. I can't move. All I can do is stare in his deep blue eyes that remind me of a cloudless day where I can see for miles. This is Keegan, the boy I have planned to marry since I was fourteen, the boy I have languished over and missed with every inch of my soul. And here he is in front of me now, in the dark, alone, and he's two inches from my face.

I understand the Greaters' laws about opposite sexes not being allowed alone. Jamie's warning about being with Fischer makes perfect sense now, only Fischer has never gotten this close before.

Pounding footsteps sound in the fog, and we snap out of our trance. I look at Keegan nervously, confused.

He pulls me behind a set of trees.

"They were spotted coming from the riverboat," the guard says into his tiny computer as he passes us. "The spotter said there were about a dozen in all."

I just catch my gasp before it escapes. Someone saw us! I look up at Keegan with wide eyes. His nostrils flare, and he breathes deep.

Another set of running feet approaches from our street. What if the guards don't stop coming? How will we ever get home without being caught?

The two guards meet up somewhere out of our line of sight. "We got the old man, the leader. He's dead," one guard says.

I cover my mouth to keep from crying out. Keegan puts his arms around me and pulls me to his chest. "We'll be fine," he whispers.

"Who spotted them?" the second guard asks.

"Some girl," the first one says. "I think her name was Lil or something. A student."

Lil? Not Lilith. It couldn't be. Is that why she's been so nice to me? So she could get close to spy on me? I feel sick.

The first guard's computer beeps, and he speaks into it. "They got two guys," he says.

Two people have been captured? What about Fischer? What will they do to him? What if they send him back to his Lesser city? Will I ever see him again?

I won't even be able to check until tomorrow after my Test, which almost seems like a joke at this point.

The guards disappear over the levy and we wait for an eternity.

Finally Keegan moves to check the path. "It's clear. If we're going to go, we better go now."

I nod, cold without his body heat surrounding me.

"Should we split up?" I ask. "So that both of us don't get caught?"

"No way. I'm not leaving you."

We sneak into the darkness and check the road. Fog drifts ominously down the street, and I wonder if we'd even see the guards.

"Let's go," Keegan says. We bolt across the street and hurry through the backyards until we reach my back porch.

Panic rises in me at the thought of going inside and this night being over. How can I lay down and rest when Mr. Elders is dead and Fischer might have been caught? My throat feels swollen shut and I swallow hard. "Thank you for coming with me tonight."

Keegan watches me, his eyes serious. "You don't have to thank me for being with you."

Is he going to try to kiss me now? Will I let him if he tries?

I'm relieved when he doesn't.

"I'll see you tomorrow," I say. I slip into my house and immediately peek through the window to make sure he gets to his own yard.

When he's out of sight I go to bed, but sleep doesn't come. Tomorrow I will take my Test, and only after that will I find out whether Fischer is safe. Tomorrow my life may change forever.

44

The testing center is near the universities. I've come to this part of the city a handful of times, whenever I was visiting Mom or Dad at work, which wasn't often. All fifty of the graduating students from school are there. Easton sits wringing his thumbs together. A boy beside him says something, seeming to draw him out of his own private hell. Easton doesn't respond, only leans over and puts his elbows on his knees. The boy moves away, and Easton's alone again.

We sit in the large waiting area, a few making nervous chatter, but mostly silent. Some of the boys recognize Keegan and pelt him with questions about who he's met and what he's done while away.

The boy from last night is here, too. I'm surprised, because Markus and Ava are a year younger than me, so I assumed the boy was the same age. His presence makes my stomach drop, because that just makes it all the more likely that Fischer was caught.

Lilith sits alone in the corner. She doesn't look up, but she must have noticed I'm here. Everyone has made a big fuss over Keegan, and there's no way she missed it.

Is she surprised to see me? Does she feel guilty?

Should I confront her?

I look away, my decision made. I need to focus on my Test. I didn't even glance at the pamphlet they handed out after graduation. I was too occupied with meeting Fischer's group and helping Mom. What should I expect? They'll probably ask me questions about my interests. My hobbies. My loyalties.

I swallow my panic. What will I say? Will I lie?

Hours tick away. One by one, other kids are called back. There doesn't seem to be any set order for the Tests, they just call names randomly.

"You'll do fine," Keegan says, breaking me out of my musings. "I didn't even try, and I still made Middle."

I try to smile, but it comes off as more of a grimace. I wipe my sweaty palms on my pants and shift in my seat. "Why don't they just call me already?"

"They will," he says.

Almost like he's made my request come true himself, a woman in a crisp blue blouse and gray pencil skirt appears. I only know what a pencil skirt is because once Jamie bought a book of old fashioned clothing trends from two hundred years ago.

"Hana Norfolk?"

It's about time. "I'm here."

She leads me to the end of a long hallway. "Here we are," she says smiling, completely at ease.

"Thanks," I mumble.

She opens the door to let me in, and then closes it behind me. The sound of the door clicking into place behind me sets my veins pumping and I spin around to clutch at the knob. Locked.

That really, really stinks.

The room is quiet, and I move like lava to see what awaits me. I expect a table or at least a desk, and then the test giver, of course. There's a clock on one wall, and it's set to the wrong time. It reads nine o'clock.

There is one chair—a hard, metal chair—and a

podium with a woman behind it. She's wearing glasses and a dark business suit. Her dark hair is pulled into a tight knob at the base of her neck, but her hair is unlike any I've seen before. It sparkles, almost like fire but more dancing, more glimmering.

I stand glued in place watching her glittering head.

"Won't you sit down?" Her voice is flat and stern, not welcoming and inquisitive.

I clear my throat and look away. Strange or not, it is probably rude to stare at your tester, not to mention kind of stupid. I hurry to the chair and slide into place.

"State your name."

"Hana Norfolk."

"Proposed occupation?"

"Government work."

She makes marks on something she has on the podium, but I don't see a pen in her hand so I'm not sure what she's writing. I lean forward, trying my best to see.

She glances at me and narrows her eyes. "Did you need something?"

I get the impression she isn't as open to questions as other people I've met. I sit back. "Not really."

She frowns, but keeps speaking. "Tell me about a usual day in the life of Hana Norfolk."

It's something in her eyes that sets my pulse to throbbing again. An iciness. A chill. An implied knowledge.

I take a deep breath. I can do this. "Well, before graduation I went to school every day, and after school I went to visit my mom in the hospital. She has the mutation."

Tap tap tap on whatever she's got on that podium.

My tester doesn't even glance at me.

"Go on."

I force my eyes away. "After visiting her I go home and cook dinner for me and my dad. School has only been out for two days, so I haven't really had a chance to change my routine much."

Tap tap.

Finally, she looks at me. Right in the eye. "That's it? There are no special friends you spend time with?"

Heat floods my face and chest and stomach. I don't know for sure, but it feels like she's baiting me. Who does she want me to talk about? Jamie?

Maybe she's referring to Ava or Fischer or Keegan.

I swallow hard. "I have a handful of friends I do things with every now and then."

She rolls her eyes and sighs. "In case you haven't figured it out yet, I would like you to elaborate."

Tap tap tap. Only this time it's my toe tapping the floor in a quick rhythm. "My best friend Keegan is home on break, and I've spent the last few days with him. Before that I hung out with a couple of other friends—Jamie and Ava. But not very often since my mom got sick."

"And how are Jamie and Ava?"

My anger simmers and boils and erupts. She was baiting me. "I couldn't say for sure, as they've both been taken away."

She watches me, not confirming or denying or seeming to care one single iota.

I keep eye contact until I can't take it anymore.

A tiny smile turns up the corners of her mouth, and she glances back at her podium. "Tell me why you want to work in government."

I tell her about my ideas for helping the Lessers,

and the reasons I think this will benefit our country.

She *tap tap taps* again.

I fidget fidget fidget.

"Did your mother ever speak with you about her military work?"

My hands still. "What?"

"Your mother was a top military official before she became a professor at the military academy. Did she ever tell you about her time in that position?"

My mom became a professor sometime around my eighth birthday. I don't remember much about her job before then, and I definitely didn't know she was a top official. "No. She never mentioned it to me at all."

She watches me, studies me. Finally, she nods and goes back to tapping. Obviously, she's decided I'm not lying.

"Tell me about all the times you've been caught out after curfew."

Thankfully, she looks away, letting me bask in my shock in peace. I wasn't expecting to talk about that. I could deny it, but what good would that do? "I was caught out once when I came home from visiting my mom at the hospital, and another time when I—I snuck out to meet a friend."

She nods and taps and then looks back to me. "Any other times you want to elaborate on?"

I refuse to look away. "No."

She gives a sharp nod. "Very well. You know we don't take kindly to lawbreakers, correct?"

Swallow. "I'm aware."

"Excellent. I think I have all I need for now. You may go."

I stay in my chair, unsure if she means it.

She glances up from the podium. "What are you

waiting for?"

I stand, my knees wobbling. "Sorry," I say. I hurry toward the door.

"Oh, Miss Norfolk? Don't speak of your test with anyone."

Now even my hands are shaking, but thankfully, the door has been unlocked. I hurry into the hall and rush back toward Keegan.

That didn't go well. I may be seeing Jamie again after all.

45

Keegan grins at me when I rejoin him in the lobby. "Didn't I tell you it would be fine?"

I smile and shrug a little. I don't know what to say. Confiding in him isn't an option, and it's not like I have much to discuss. What would I say? I blew my shot at a decent future? I never thought about that as I sneaked out to meet Fischer all those times.

We walk into the bright sunlight. It warms my arms, but not my shaking nerves.

Kids skip down the side walk, sweaters tied around their waists, laughing and smiling into the sun.

I shiver and wrap my arms around my chest.

"Are you cold?" Keegan asks.

"Just anxious, I guess." We're on our way to the hospital now. I'll get to see Mom and tell her the things I've learned about God.

I close my eyes and take a deep breath. The warm air feels good in my lungs and calms me. I have to push the Test out of my thoughts for now. Being able to tell Mom about God makes the thought of being demoted easier to take.

Besides that, at the hospital I'll get to see whether or not Fischer was captured last night. What if he isn't at the hospital?

I can't voice my concerns to Keegan. He won't understand. In fact, it will be the opposite. He'll be angry. Jealous.

Confusion swirls around inside my head. Keegan or Fischer? Fischer or Keegan? Last night I was so sure I wanted Keegan to kiss me. I've imagined what it would feel like a thousand times. But Fischer has made me all but forget Keegan. I think about Fischer all the time now, but do I ever dream of him kissing me?

"You look awfully sad for someone who just aced her Test," Keegan says with a smile.

I force a smile and look away. I don't want him to see my watery eyes. "Aren't you at all affected by last night?" I ask. It hits me that if the Greaters know about everything I've been doing, what about the others? Do they know about Keegan's involvement last night?

I shiver again and glance at him as he answers.

"I'm trying not to think about it too much. Not yet. I'll think about it when it's quiet, and when I can find my own answers."

I gladly let my mind switch gears. "How will you find answers like that on your own?" What if he doesn't choose the right way? According to what Mr. Elders said, not choosing God means rejecting him.

My stomach twists at the thought of Mr. Elders. Dead.

"Don't worry about me, Hana. I'm a big boy."

We reach the hospital and Keegan stops short. He looks up at the tall building. "I've never been in a hospital before."

"It's not so bad," I say. "Of course, it's not as fantastic as lights on a stage or a speaker that blares music to everyone for miles around, but there are actually lights that stay on all day. It took me a while to get used to that."

He smiles tightly, clearly uncomfortable.

I lay my hand on his arm. "It'll be fine. It's just

Mom. She looks different, but she's the same. We told her you were here, and she's thrilled to see you."

I'm still holding his arm, and heat rushes to my cheeks and ears. I pull my hand away.

He doesn't even pretend to not see my embarrassment. Instead, he watches my eyes. His are open, wide, hopeful. He smiles a little. "I know. Besides, I'd follow you anywhere."

My heart stutters, but to cover it up I push through the doors.

We jog up to the third floor and immediately chaos hits me. Medics run through the hall grabbing things. Someone yells from down the hall.

I frown and glance toward Mom's room. A crowd has gathered.

I cry out and run as fast as I can. My heart pounds in beat with my footsteps. I haven't told her yet. She doesn't know about God. She can't be dead.

"What's happening?" I demand.

Dr. Lane looks distraught as she flips through Mom's chart spastically, like she can't believe what she's seeing and is looking for what will clear it up.

"It's for the best," Dr. Bentford says. He moves to put his hand on Dr. Lane's shoulder.

She pushes him off and keeps flipping through the chart.

My dad stands to the side, tears streaming down his face.

"What's going on?" I say again.

"They're taking her away," Dad says.

"What?"

My dad covers his face with his hands, his shoulders shaking. "Her medical allowance ran out."

Dr. Bentford moves forward and puts his hand on

my back.

I jerk away from him like he's on fire. "Don't touch me!"

His face turns to stone. "Her medical allowance has run out. The word came a few minutes ago, and that's all there is to it. She will be moved to the Lesser hospital, where she will receive further treatment."

A few minutes ago? The breath rushes out of me. I can't believe this is happening. I can't believe all these years I've bought into their lie, always believing that the Greaters took care of us.

"She's a faithful citizen," I say. "A loyal citizen. How can you do this to her?"

My dad cries silently, tears slipping down his cheeks, his shoulders shaking.

Two medics prepare a fresh bed for her in the hallway. My mom lays lifeless in her room, and I rush to her. Her cheeks are sunken in, and her eyes have dark circles around them.

"Mom?"

Her eyes flutter open, but it looks like they'll close again any second.

"Mom, you have to listen to me," I say. Everyone has backed out of the room, giving me privacy I guess. If only they knew what I was going to say. "I know about God, Mom. I found out what happens when you die. Can you understand me?"

She watches me closely and squeezes my hand. It's so weak it feels no firmer than a butterfly's wings.

"God is real, and He loves us. All of us. He wants us all to have eternal life with Him, in Heaven, but we have to ask Him for it. Can you do that, Mom? It's called praying." The words still feel foreign on my tongue, and I stutter over the last sentence.

Her squeeze is more forceful this time. She nods slightly.

Does she really understand so quickly? But then I remember that she was already looking for answers. She knows things from what she's heard over the years. Relief chokes me, and tears swell in my eyes. "Just ask Him, Mom. Just like that. I'll pray with you." I try to reword the prayer Fischer prayed with me. My mom's lips move almost imperceptibly, but she does it. She's praying with me.

I can't stop the tears that spill over my cheeks. I did it. I got to her in time. After all the struggles, the chemo rejection, the arrests, I've helped her in some way. "Thank you, God," I say.

Fischer steps into the room and pulls me aside. "You have to let them go, Hana. We can't stop them."

"Why not send her home?" I ask. I work to control my voice. "She won't live in the Lesser hospital long—you know that as well as I do. Why can't she come home and spend the rest of her time in peace?"

Dr. Bentford steps in and shakes his head. "I'm sorry. That's not the way things are done."

The way things are done? What does it matter if she dies in the Lesser hospital or at home? And then it hits me. They can do whatever they want with her in the Lesser hospital. We can't visit her. They will be accountable to no one. If she comes home, they'd have to give her allowances. Sending her to a Lesser hospital is sending her away to die quickly.

My anger snaps as cleanly as a fishing line. I charge into the hall. "You're liars. You're all liars. Give her the chemo drugs, you monsters! I know you have them. I saw her chart! I heard you talking about them!"

My dad stops crying and stares at me in shock.

Dr. Lane's head snaps up and her eyes are wide. Dr. Bentford watches me warily.

Fischer puts his hand on my shoulder, and I shrug it off. "I know what you do. You're monsters and murderers! I won't stop. I won't stop until the truth comes out."

Fischer drags me away, but I don't stop. "You kill anyone who is no longer profitable to the Greaters. Human life doesn't matter to you. Money does. You're monsters! You'll be accountable to God one day. You'll have to answer for the souls you sent to hell! Give her the chemo drugs. Give them to her!"

I'm around the corner now and Fischer shakes me by the shoulders. "You have to stop, Hana. You have to stop *now*! You've said too much. Way too much." He rubs a hand over his face.

The fight goes out of me, and I collapse to the cold, tile floor. A Lesser. They're demoting Mom to Lesser because she has the mutation. She can't help it! It's not her fault. They're the ones who might be able to fix her. They're choosing not to help. Instead, they're sending her away to die.

Dr. Lane's face appears in front of mine. "That was a very stupid thing you did back there."

I look up at her and shoot her with all the contempt I can muster. "Are you really going to lecture me?" I wipe my nose with the back of my hand. I hope it disgusts her.

She shakes her head. "No. It was brave—not to mention true—but it was still stupid. It's not time for a full frontal war. There are casualties in every battle. Unfortunately, your mom is going to be one of them. But we will win, if we keep our heads. If *you* keep *your* head. Spouting stuff like that will only get you demoted yourself, and what good can you do, locked away in a Lesser community?"

Now it's my turn to stare in shock at Dr. Lane. A realization hits me. "You gave her the Bible verse."

She doesn't respond to that. "Do you understand what I said?"

"Yes."

"Good." She stands up and strides away.

"You need to say goodbye to your mom," Fischer says softly. "You'll regret it if you don't."

I swallow hard. "OK."

He takes me by the hand and leads me back down the hall. I wonder if anyone notices we're holding hands, and then I think how strange it is that I would even think of that at a time like this.

Mom lies with her eyes closed in the new bed they've prepared. Dr. Bentford scowls at me as I approach, but I ignore him.

Her chest rises and falls softly. I wonder if she'll even make it through the night. "Mom?" She doesn't turn and look at me, but I can tell she's listening. "I love you, Mom. I love you so much."

That's all I can say.

Then her lips move, so softly I barely notice. "There's more," she whispers.

"What Mom? What did you say?" I lean in close, but she doesn't speak again.

Eventually, I feel someone's arms on me, gently tugging me away. I am enveloped in a hug, and I recognize Dad's scent. We both cry.

"It's best if you leave before we do the transport. It will be easier that way." It's Dr. Bentford's voice. He still sounds wary, like he's waiting for me to argue.

I don't. Instead, I leave the hospital wordlessly. I

won't fight with him today, or maybe ever. But there will be a fight. Somewhere down the line, when the day is right, there will be a war.

46

I sit with Dad and Keegan in my living room. I've cried all the tears I have, but Dad still sniffles.

Keegan offers me a tissue and I wipe my face. There's a growing pile of the little white wisps beside me.

"Maybe they'll let you visit her," Keegan says.

My dad shakes his head. "No. Middles aren't allowed to go into Lesser cities. Ever."

His words strike me. "Middles can't go in, but can Lessers travel between cities like Middles can?"

My dad shrugs. "I suppose so."

"That's good."

"Good?" Keegan asks.

The woman told me not to talk about the Test, but at this point I don't care what they do to me. If they demote me, then at least I'll be able to find Mom and Jamie. "I'm not supposed to tell you about my Test today," I say. "But I don't really care about their rules anymore."

"What are you saying, Hana?" Dad asks.

"I think they're going to demote me."

Keegan's mouth literally drops open, and Dad is shocked speechless.

I shift on the sofa. "The woman said they've been watching me. I guess I've been on the radar since I got arrested."

"What?" Keegan says. His eyes are huge, and he

stares at me like I've grown a second nose.

I shrug and glance nervously at Dad. I forgot I still haven't told Keegan everything that's gone on in the last few weeks.

"What were you arrested for?" he asks.

"Breaking curfew." My voice is less sure now.

"What were you doing?" he asks incredulously.

Well, I told him I'd changed, didn't I? But I know my answer is going to hurt him, even if it isn't true. I don't want Dad to know what I was really doing that night. "I was out meeting someone."

"A boy," Dad says, his nostrils flaring. He stands now. "And they've been watching you ever since?" He shakes his head, pacing the room. "No wonder they're doing this to your mother. They're punishing you."

I stare at him in shock. Demoting *me* would punish me. Why would they demote my mom to punish me?

"You blamed them back at the hospital," he says. "But it's your fault. You brought this on us." His voice is low and menacing. Hateful.

Hot tears burn my eyes and I shake my head, dumbfounded. "They denied the chemo drugs before I ever started talking to Fischer."

Regret stabs me as soon as I speak the words. The last thing I want to do is implicate Fischer, especially to Dad when he's losing his mind.

He shakes his head, glaring at me. "Get out of here."

"Dad!" I say, the tears overflowing.

Keegan puts his hand on my arm and shakes his head. He nods toward the back door and I follow him out.

The warm afternoon air doesn't comfort me. This is my fault. Had the decision already been made before

I even went to the Test? What if they decided to demote her because Dr. Bentford saw the Bible verse I left on her bedside table? I'd thought there wasn't anything worse they could do to her. Apparently, I was wrong.

Keegan wraps his arms around me and I cry into his shoulder. My body shakes as the sobs come. He holds me tighter.

"He's hurting," Keegan says. "He's lost your mom—his wife. He's angry, and he's blaming it on you. He'll change his mind, but we have to give him some time."

I don't speak. I just let him hold me while I cry. How can I admit that it really is my fault?

He holds me around my waist with one hand and smooths my hair with the other. "It will be fine. I know."

Of course, he doesn't know. How could he? He hasn't been around, and he doesn't know what I've done. Still, his words make me feel better. I finally stop crying and sit with him in the grass. He holds my hand, stroking it lightly with his thumb.

"Is it true that you were arrested because you were trying to meet Fischer?"

My heart picks up speed, and I feel like even the world spins faster. "Not only Fischer," I say quickly. "The whole group. My dad doesn't know that, of course."

He nods. "I figured as much. What would possess you to do that?"

I glance at him quickly.

He's grinning at me. "You *have* changed, haven't you?"

I turn away from him and stare at my back door,

wishing Dad would walk through and tell me he loves me. "Yes," I say. "For the good, I hope."

"Definitely for the good, and your changes inside have changed your looks outside. You're more beautiful than ever."

I'm suddenly very aware of his hand holding mine. No one has ever called me beautiful before. My throat closes in, and I gently pull my hand from his grasp.

"There are still some rules I'm not willing to break," I say softly.

He watches me, his eyes questioning.

I can imagine what he thinks. What about Fischer? Would I break the rules for him?

But I doubt he can guess the real reason I refuse him.

Jamie.

Instead of questioning me, he leans away. "So tell me about your Test."

Chills race down my arm and I shiver. "They locked me in a room."

"What?"

"They locked me in a room," I say with a shrug. The grass beneath my fingers is smooth and soft. I rub it slowly, enjoying its neutral presence in my life. "I sat in a cold, metal chair while my tester stood in front of me tapping on some type of small machine."

"My Test wasn't like that at all," Keegan says, looking up at the blue sky.

"Yeah, well, you didn't go breaking a bunch of laws I guess."

His eyes meet mine dead on. He watches me for what feels like ever, and then he turns away.

47

Keegan sits with me until it gets dark. My dad is nowhere to be seen, so I assume he left. I don't understand how he could blame me, but I try to remember what Keegan said. I can only hope he'll come around. I have to admit I haven't made it easy on him—sneaking out after curfew and messing around with illegal religion.

But what if he doesn't come around? What if he never forgives me, and worse, what if he never believes in God?

Keegan and I say goodbye, and he promises to come first thing in the morning. I lay on my bed with a sigh. Is there anything I can do for Dad? I don't know, but maybe Fischer will.

Fischer.

I smile, because I realize now he wasn't caught. It didn't register at the hospital, but now I let the warm relief wash over me.

What will Fischer think of my Test?

Fear boils in my stomach for the first time. What would demotion bring? I considered it with Jamie, but this is different. This is me.

I haven't heard Dad return, and worry creeps into my thoughts. I let Fischer's name slip, and with Dad in such a rage, what if he's gone to the guards to tell them?

I need to see Fischer, to make sure he's OK.

Besides, I want to ask him how Mom did after we left.

I'm not sure when I make the decision, but before I know it I'm dressed all in black and I slip out the back door. I almost expect guards to be patrolling my house on a regular basis, but the street looks empty enough. They must figure if they're demoting me anyway it doesn't matter all that much. Adrenaline shoots through my limbs as I weave in and out of alleys. I'm not even sure where I'm going until I find myself heading toward the education district, toward the university dormitories.

A sliver of a moon dots the sky, and I'm thankful for the darkness. I reach the university campuses and hurry onto the huge lawns.

Laughter drifts on the breeze and I freeze. I slip behind a tree just as a couple sneaks past. Hands clasped, they giggle into each other's faces. They can't be so foolish, can they? Don't they know they'll get caught?

But then I hear more laughter, louder this time. Two guys, obviously students, toss a football across a lawn. The more I look, the more I see. Students are everywhere!

Don't they have curfews? Do the students have different rules? Obviously, they do. This is something I'll have to ask Keegan or Fischer about.

What little fear I have of the Greaters fades away, and I walk boldly across the lawn toward the dorms.

I reach the first tall dormitory building and the stupidity of my plan hits me. How am I going to find Fischer? Go door to door?

I rub my eyes, weary from a long day. The thought of everything that's happened today overwhelms me. My Test, possible demotion, and Mom. "Mom," I whisper. My lip quivers, and I stubbornly bite it. Pain shoots through the sensitive, soft skin, but it doesn't matter. I won't cry or mourn. I will find her instead.

I square my shoulders and march into the first building. Narrow hallways and doors line the space, and a wide staircase leads to the next floor. Dim lights glow down the hall, casting shadows on the people inside. I notice something about this dorm—it's full of girls. Some hold hands, others laugh together. Smoke lingers in the air, and many of the girls pass dark bottles around.

I hurry outside, sure Fischer won't be in this building. Obviously, the dorms are separated into buildings for guys and girls.

The fresh air doesn't help get the disturbing images out of my head, though. I wrap my arms around my stomach and start looking for someone who can help me.

A couple comes from the bushes, giggling and holding hands.

"Excuse me, which building is the boys' dorm?"

The couple stops and the boy watches me. His eyes scan me from head to toe. I have to force myself not to run away. "It's that building over there," he says, nodding behind me.

"Thanks," I mutter, glad to hurry away.

It's much louder in the boys' building. Guys jog up and down the stairs, some shout, and others wrestle in the floor.

A group near the door hushes when I walk in. At first they just stare at me, but then one brave soul steps over to me. "Do you need something, honey?"

At first I think he's serious, but then he breaks into a barking laugh. His buddies howl with giggles, too.

"I'm looking for Fischer—," I freeze. Fischer who? I realize I don't know. I've come all this way and I don't even know his last name.

By now most of the guys on the first floor have noticed I'm there. Despite the couples roaming out in the lawn, it looks like most of the students keep the rule about not being alone with the opposite sex.

The din quiets, and they stare.

"Fischer who?" the first guy asks. "You can call me Fischer if you want." More uncontrolled laughter.

"He's a medical student," I say, raising my voice above the noise. "He works at the hospital."

The boy puts his hand over his heart. "You're breaking me, honey. Tell me you want me."

Words escape me—I've never been the wittiest person at school. Instead, I shake my head.

"Are you talking about Bible boy?" someone calls out.

Some of the other guys groan.

"Bible boy has a girl coming over?" another guy shouts. A few people whistle, but the first guy answers.

"He's in room 314. Third floor."

"Thanks," I say, weaving in and out of bodies to get to the stairs.

"Save a little for me!" he calls.

I don't acknowledge him and by the time I've reached the third floor, I notice the raucous downstairs is louder than ever.

Room 314 glares at me. Am I bold enough to just knock on his door?

Suddenly my brave plan seems awfully stupid. After all the secret meetings Fischer has gone to, after all the careful plans, I'm going to put him in jeopardy by showing up at his door. This is probably the stupidest thing I've done yet.

I knock.

Shuffling comes from behind the door, and a moment later the door opens a crack. A curly-headed guy stands behind it. "Can I help you?"

"I'm looking for Fischer."

He studies me for a long moment and finally shrugs. "He's not here. Didn't come home after his shift at the hospital."

Everything else fades away. All I can think is that Dad turned him in. Fischer is gone.

"He didn't come home? Are you sure?"

The big guy chuckles. "Yeah, I'm pretty sure I'm in this room by myself."

I hesitate, shuffling my feet back and forth. "OK, thanks."

The roommate shuts the door before I even walk away, and now I face going back to the snake pit below. I fight tears that threaten to break from my eyes. Can I sneak out without anyone noticing?

Doubtful.

Then another idea hits me. I take the steps two at a time to the second floor and find a window at the end of the hall. It slides up easily, and the warm night air hits me in the face. It's the perfect time of year—not too hot or too cold, and the night air is comfortable. Enjoyable.

I stick my head out the window and look for a way down. The first floor of the building is old brick. Most of the bricks are cracked at best and crumbling at worst, but there's a ledge of brick where it meets the plastic siding that covers the upper floors.

I step out on the ledge, willing my knees to stop shaking. I inch my way to the corner of the building.

There's a rain spout, and a row of overgrown bushes at the bottom. If I make it to the rain spout I can climb down. If I slip, at least the bushes will break my fall.

My heart beats like footsteps pounding down the sidewalk, but then I realize it *is* footsteps pounding down the sidewalk.

I'm almost at the corner when I glance at the runner.

Fischer's face frowns up at me. "Hana! What are you doing?"

Before I can call out his name, I slip.

The bushes break my fall, but I hit the ground with a thud, branches drawing blood from my arms and face. I try inhaling, but my lungs won't work.

The ability to breathe comes back like a rushing wind, and so does the pain.

I cry out, and Fischer is there.

"My foot," I say. "I think I broke it."

"Open your mouth," he says.

"What?" Is he crazy?

"Just do it."

I open it and something hard and rough meets my tongue. A piece of wood? He stuck a piece of wood in my mouth to keep me quiet.

"Bite down," he says. "It will help with the pain."

I give it a try. It actually works.

"What are you doing here?" he asks. He glances at the stick in my mouth and shakes his head. "Never mind, you can tell me later."

His hands gently probe my ankle and foot, barely grazing my skin.

I can't help but notice how warm his fingers are on my skin.

"I think you need to go to the hospital."

Panic rises up my throat, and I shake my head furiously.

"I'm not saying you should go, just that you need to. I wouldn't want to go there if I were you either. I can wrap it for now, but eventually you're going to need it looked at. I can probably get you some pain medicine."

He sits back on his heels and looks up. "I can't take you in through all those guys, but I can't leave you out here, either."

There's no more doubt that this is the dumbest thing I've ever done.

"Can you put any weight on it?" he asks. He scrambles to his feet and offers me a hand.

I reach a shaky hand toward him and he tugs. I heave myself up with a grunt. My head spins and my stomach rolls. I turn to the bushes and retch.

I can't believe I'm throwing up in front of Fischer.

"It's OK," he says softly. He pulls the short hair away from my face, his fingertips grazing my neck.

I shiver and quickly wipe my mouth with my sleeve so he won't notice. "I'm sorry," I say. "I was trying to find you. You weren't home, and I didn't want to go back through the people downstairs."

He frowns.

I love being the one who makes him smile, but I hate being the one who makes him frown.

"It was dumb. I have no problem admitting it."

He smiles a little. "Yeah? OK, let's see if I can help you walk. We'll never make it to your house unnoticed though, I'm just warning you."

The dread is back. "Let me go alone. I don't want to get you in trouble."

He ignores me and pulls my arm across his

shoulders. "See if you can take a step."

"Ow!" I cry out, pain ripping through my leg. "No, I can't."

He pauses. "I don't know what to do."

This isn't the Fischer I know. He always thinks of something—always has a plan. He's calm and methodical and smart. He'll think of something.

After a moment he looks at me, his eyes unsure. "I have an idea."

48

The car's engine purrs softly as Fischer helps me inside. "Are you sure about this? Won't a car draw more attention than just walking?" Already kids on campus are staring at us, their eyes wide with questions, confusion, and jealousy. Not many people get to ride in cars.

"Well, if you could walk we wouldn't be borrowing Westin's car in the first place." It's the closest I've ever heard him come to losing his patience.

Westin is Fischer's roommate, and he's from our city. Fischer hid me behind the car while he went inside to beg Westin for the favor.

"It'll be fine," he assures me. "It's not like a guard can catch us on foot. If anyone shows up at your house, we'll deal with it. What else are we supposed to do?"

I know he's right, but I don't like it.

He shuts the door softly behind me, and I lay across the back seat so no one will see us in the car together. The seat is covered in a sticky plastic, and my skin peels off it as I shift. The ceiling of the car is drooped in material, and the entire car smells like a dirty shoe.

Most cars didn't survive the disasters, and no new ones have been built since then except a few that have been re-built by car buffs who use their entertainment allowance to build things.

Fischer climbs in the driver's seat, and we gently

start forward.

"Have you ever driven before?"

His silence answers my question pretty well.

"I've never even been inside a car this nice," I say. "This isn't so bad." And it isn't. I thought it would be loud and bumpy like the police car, but it's fairly quiet and smooth. The roads are broken and pocked with holes, though, and every jostle sends pain shooting up my leg.

"We're pulling off campus and onto the regular streets now," he warns. "I'll tell you if I see any guards."

We drive in silence for a few minutes before he asks, "Why did you come to find me?"

Is he asking because he wants a tangible reason, or because he wants an emotional one? I haven't figured out the emotional one myself. "My dad was gone, and it was after curfew. He blames me for Mom getting sent away. He says it was because I was being watched, and they saw me breaking laws. I needed to talk to someone, and I wanted to make sure you were OK." It hits me that I might have just asked Keegan to stay, but all I could think of at the time was that Fischer was safe. I bite my lip. Does that mean I chose Fischer over Keegan?

"Your dad came to see me at the hospital," Fischer says. "That's why I got home late."

"What?" I can't imagine Dad going to see Fischer. Did Dad hit him? Yell at him? Threaten to turn him in?

"He wanted to know more details about your mom, and he told me what he'd said to you. He also asked me to stay away from you. I'm afraid he's not going to be very happy when he sees us together."

"No, probably not." My mind races with questions

of my own. "How was Mom?"

"She was at peace. She didn't question them or put up a fight."

His answer makes me feel better and worse all at the same time. Was she too weak to put up a fight? Or was she truly at peace? "What will happen to her now, Fischer? Will she die?" I bite my lip, trying not to cry.

He's quiet for what feels like ever. "I don't know."

"What about my dad? He doesn't believe in God." I can't stop the tears now.

"You have to pray for him," Fischer says. His eyes watch me in the little mirror on the glass above his head. "You can ask God to show your dad the way."

I look away from the mirror. More praying. That seems like something I'll have to get used to—kind of like touching people took some adjusting.

"Is it true what your dad said about your Test? Did they say they were going to demote you?"

"I'm not sure," I say. Guilt burns my stomach like acid. "She didn't say it exactly, but I got that impression."

He doesn't say anything, but I can see him in the mirror. His mouth is set in a straight line, and his forehead is wrinkled. Does he blame me, too, or maybe he blames himself?

Fischer doesn't speak for long, excruciating minutes. When he finally speaks, his words are so soft I can barely hear them. "It's not your fault." He pauses, and then says, "There's a guard watching us approach. It looks like she's reporting us in her communicator."

I bite back my tears. "Will we get in trouble?"

"We *are* out past curfew," he says. "But we're almost to your house."

The car slows down and Fischer helps me out.

Pain shoots up my leg again and I gasp.

"Let's get you inside," he says softly. "Then I can wrap your foot."

We hobble up the steps to my house, our arms tangled around each other. I've never been so warm in my life.

Fischer stops just before we open the door. He looks at me, his brown eyes serious and intense. "I understand, Hana. And it's OK."

I stare into those eyes and tears sting my own. He doesn't hate me, and he isn't blaming me.

He reaches up, hesitantly, softly, and brushes a strand of hair from my face. "Are you ready?"

My knees shake, but I nod. We push inside.

Frost Moon, our country's Great Supreme, sits on the couch with Dad, and we stop.

The atmosphere is like a vacuum. My dad's lips are thin and white, and Fischer and I stand frozen, his arm around my waist and my arm around his shoulders. What kind of picture do we paint, the two of us intertwined?

Frost Moon is the only one who doesn't seem at all upset. "Ah, here's the lady I seek. Are you injured, Hana?"

Fischer snaps into action. "She fell. I think her foot may be broken."

My dad hurries to help me onto the couch. The pain is worse than before, but I bite back a cry as they settle me in. My dad returns to his seat as Fischer shoves his hands in his pockets and steps back, discomfort and uncertainty written all over his face.

"Have you seen a doctor?" Frost Moon asks.

I shake my head, too afraid to speak. Why is he here? Did Dad report me after all? Have they come to take me away?

I tell myself to calm down. Frost Moon didn't come for Jamie's demotion. The Great Supreme is here for something else.

He pulls a letter from his suit coat. Even this late at night he wears a full dress suit of black with white pinstripes. "I came to bring you your Test results, but it appears it will have to wait until we get you looked at." He glances at Fischer. "Well, Medic, what can you do for her?"

My mind reels that Frost Moon not only sits in my living room wanting to speak to me, but also that he knows Fischer.

Fischer steps forward. "I was going to wrap it for her."

Frost Moon waves his hand magnanimously. "Be my guest."

"Do you have a wrap?" Fischer asks Dad. Most houses keep simple first aid kits, since getting to the hospital in and of itself is a hassle.

My dad springs from his seat, obviously glad to have something to do. "It's in the upstairs closet."

His feet pound up the steps and Frost Moon turns to me.

"When I arrived to deliver your Test results, Hana, your dad was quite distraught that you weren't home. Care to elaborate?"

His eyes are open. Honest. Masked. This is the man who allowed Mom to be sent away. I won't bow to him.

"No."

His eyebrows shoot up just as Dad comes back downstairs. "Here it is," he says.

Fischer kneels in front of me and begins working

on my foot. My dad watches Fischer closely, but Frost Moon watches me.

I don't back down. I refuse to. He's enabled the people I love to be sent away, and then came here to give me my Test results like I should be happy to see him.

When Fischer finishes he steps away, and all eyes turn to Frost Moon. He doesn't disappoint.

"Miss Hana Norfolk, you have exceeded all expectations. It is rare indeed for one to Test higher than their original standing. Your medic here can tell you that much." He glances briefly at Fischer and then back to me. Confusion clutters up my head. Testing above one's station?

"We have been watching you for many, many years. You've shown great potential for being a leader, and you have reached a coveted place where you will be in the position to get help to those who need it most." He glances at Dad. "You must get it from your mother. Hana, do you understand what I'm saying?"

His icy eyes drill into mine. Is he saying what I think he's saying? Because it sounds like he's saying I'm not being demoted.

"Of course, with great privilege comes a responsibility. You have information I would like."

I glance at Dad. His gaze is on his shoes, like the information being given is everyday stuff. I don't look at Fischer. Frost Moon doesn't need to know that Fischer plays into any of this, and I don't want Fischer to worry I'm going to give away his people.

The Great Supreme steps forward and hands me the letter. I take it with shaking hands.

"Hana Norfolk," he says in a firm and superior voice. "You are officially a Greater."

Don't miss the rest of the ENSLAVED series

The Blinders are off. The Choice has been Made.

DELIVERANCE,
Book Two

Hana is Greater. It's a future she never envisioned for herself, but she's not about to ignore the opportunity she's been given--the opportunity to find answers about her Mom, Jamie, and Fischer. This could be an opportunity to tell others the truth about God and uncover the secrets the Great Supreme has been keeping from their small, struggling nation.

When Hana's search brings her to the mysterious prison she's only heard of in rumors, the desire to get inside drives her to dig deeper for answers, but what she uncovers may be bigger than them all.

Can she save herself and the others before the Great Supreme realizes what she's doing, or will she give up everyone she loves in her quest for the truth?

Freedom is Within Reach, but is it at too High a Cost

REDEEMER,
Book Three

In this final chapter of the Enslaved series, Hana is faced not only with a new life, but an entirely new way of thinking. Unexpected friends give insight into who the Greaters truly are. Deciding what to do with this information sends Hana on what may be her very last journey. Ever.

Watch the book video:
http://youtu.be/e1q3Fg06I0A

Thank you for purchasing this Watershed Books title.
For other inspirational stories, please visit our on-line
bookstore at www.pelicanbookgroup.com.

For questions or more information, contact us at
customer@pelicanbookgroup.com.

Watershed Books
Make a Splash!™
an imprint of Pelican Ventures Book Group
www.PelicanBookGroup.com

Connect with Us
www.facebook.com/Pelicanbookgroup
www.twitter.com/pelicanbookgrp

To receive news and specials, subscribe to our bulletin
http://pelink.us/bulletin

May God's glory shine through
this inspirational work of fiction.

AMDG